MW01611070

MURDER IN WHITE LACE

A BRIDAL SHOP COZY MYSTERY

KAREN SUE WALKER

LARAGRAY PRESS

Copyright © 2016 by Karen Sue Walker

All rights reserved.

Published by Laragray Press

No part of this book may be reproduced in any form or by any electronic or mechanical means without written permission from the author, except for the use of brief quotations in a book review.

This is a work of fiction. All names, characters, locales, and incidents are products of the author's imagination and any resemblance to actual people, places, or events is coincidental.

For more information about me and all my books or to contact me, visit http://karensuewalker.com.

CHAPTER 1

*a*s Max Walters walked barefoot in the sand, breathing in the sea air, her busy thoughts began to settle and focus. Fluffy, cotton candy clouds floated leisurely by, as unrushed as the people strolling on the beach.

"Hi, Maxine!"

Max Walters greeted the woman passing her on the beach, not bothering to correct her even though her name wasn't short for Maxine or anything else. Her mother claimed she was named after Max Planck, the famous physicist, and her father said he named her after Maxfield Parrish, the painter. Max always suspected they thought they were having a boy, but they would never admit it.

After the neighbor updated Max on the status of her rose garden, Max returned to her task--searching for sea glass among the sand and pebbles.

A flash of red caught her eye, and she reached down between the seaweed to retrieve the rarest of sea glass.

She grabbed it before a wave hid it in its bubbly froth, and then hurried back to the damp hard sand.

She stared at the stone in her hand. Sea glass was usually worn by the sand and waves to a weathered finish. This was definitely not sea glass. This was clear and faceted, and she wondered if it had fallen out of someone's ring. After staring at it for a while, she put it in her pocket along with the five pieces of sea glass she'd discovered this morning.

She walked as far south as she could until the rocky cliff met the sea and boulders blocked her path. At the age of eight or ten, she would climb like a mountain goat over the rocks to investigate the tide pools on the other side. She peered through the haze and faintly saw the hotels lining Laguna Beach. Crystal Shores sat between Laguna and Long Beach, almost unknown to anyone but locals. Those locals knew the village was a quiet retreat from the traffic and hubbub of Orange County. Decades ago, it had been an affordable retreat, but that was no longer the case. Most of the cottages along the beach had been torn down and replaced by huge modern mansions and pseudo-Mediterranean villas. How long before all the cottages in Crystal Shores were torn down?

She walked four blocks to her home, a one-bedroom apartment over her dad's garage. She opened the back door of his house into his kitchen. Grabbing a bowl out of the cupboard, she spooned some oatmeal out of the rice cooker. He always set up breakfast the night before. She poured herself a cup of coffee, took the half and half out of the refrigerator, and sat down at one end of the huge oak dining table.

"Good morning, sunshine," Richard Walters called out as he walked into the room wearing a t-shirt and baggy pajama pants with bright yellow happy faces on them.

"Hi, Dad. What are you doing up so early?" she asked. As an artist, her dad made his own schedule.

"What do you mean? It's after nine." He paused. "Oh, very funny. I was out late last night."

"On a date?" She tried to sound casual, but she didn't want to think of her dad with another woman other than her mom. Not yet. But she knew several single women had their eyes on him. And why not? With kind blue eyes (the color of Lake Michigamme, he used to tell her when she was little) and silvery highlights in his hair, she had to admit he was handsome. She had inherited those blue eyes from her dad, but not much else. At six feet tall, he towered over her 5'4" frame. She also had her mother's brown hair. She once called it mousy, and her mother had corrected her. "We have chestnut hair," she had said. At the time, Max had rolled her eyes.

"No, it wasn't a date. Not that it's any of your business," he said, pretending to be gruff. "It's your first day without Darlene," he said, changing the subject. "You ready to run the shop on your own?"

Darlene owned Wedding Belles Bridal Salon, where Max worked. Darlene was on her way to her first vacation in years, a cruise on the Mediterranean. She had fussed about leaving Max on her own, but Max had worked for her on and off since she was sixteen, which was almost ten years now. She was perfectly capable of running the shop for a week.

"I'll be fine. It'll be hectic without an assistant, though. Darlene has been advertising for an assistant for weeks. She even told me I could hire one, but I think she just said that because she was tired of me asking about it. Anyway, it's not like I have time to find someone."

"You seem to go through a lot of assistants." He took a long sip of coffee. "Darlene's not an easy woman to work for, that's for sure." He got up and scooped up a bowl of oatmeal for himself.

"Dad, I have something to tell you," Max said. She didn't want to put it off any longer.

"Sounds serious." He sat back down at the table with his oatmeal. "What is it?"

"I got a call first thing this morning from my old boss at Bissette. They've offered me a position," she said.

"Oh." He stopped with his spoon halfway to his mouth. "Looking to get your old job back?"

"No, they don't have any openings for pattern makers right now. They do need an assistant designer." She waited for his reaction.

It was a moment before he spoke. "Max, that's great! That's the job you always wanted."

"So, you're not upset about me moving back to New York?"

"Upset? Of course not!" He reached over and squeezed her hand. "Sweetie, when you moved back to help with your mom last year, I knew it was only temporary. She's been gone almost six months now. She'd want you to get on with your life. I know working in a bridal shop in Crystal Shores isn't your dream job. Besides, I can take care of myself."

She stood up and leaned over to hug him. He was the best dad ever. "The job doesn't start until May first, so I won't leave for over a month." Her new salary meant she'd be able to afford New York rent without his help. She had always relied on her parents, but she was almost 26 and it was about time to be a grown up and get by on her own.

"Of course, I'll miss you, but I'm happy for you." Her dad stood up and took his bowl to the sink. He spoke with his back to her. "Now, you'd better get to work. I have a painting to finish." She knew he didn't want her to see him get emotional, but it made her feel better to know he wasn't thrilled about her leaving.

She went out the back door, across the courtyard, and up the stairs to her apartment over the garage. While she showered, she thought about how great it would be to live in New York again. And to be a designer! Well, an assistant designer, but still. Besides, there were so many wonderful things about New York to look forward to. She could visit her favorite diner where they served the best lemon meringue pie she'd eaten in her life. She'd be making more money in the new job, so she could afford to eat out from time to time. She ate a lot of ramen noodles and macaroni and cheese when she lived there before. And that was even with her mom sending her monthly checks to help with rent.

After toweling off, she put on a pair of black slacks and her favorite teal blue sweater. She saw the red stone sitting on her dresser and put it in her pocket, thinking that maybe it would bring her good luck. Although she believed you made your own luck, she liked to think magic existed in the world. She grabbed the leather jacket her mom bought for her 21st birthday. The edges of the sleeves were worn and one of the pockets was starting to come loose, but she would wear it until it completely fell apart. She locked the front door and walked down the steps and up the path to the street.

The haze lifted early today, and the sun shone brightly. A few fluffy white clouds floated in the sky. The cool sea breeze gently caressed her cheek and she breathed in deeply. She would miss the sea air when she moved back to New York, but she couldn't wait to get back to the hustle and bustle. She walked past pastel painted cottages with perfectly tended flowerbeds. She strolled down Rose Street, which she thought was appropriately named as she noticed a beautiful peach colored rose. She reached down to smell it.

"Stopping to smell the roses, I see." An older man was walking a tiny white dog.

She tried to remember his name but couldn't. Of course, she remembered the dog's. "Hi, Sparky," she said and reached down to pet the little Maltese.

She continued her walk, greeting an elderly woman

pruning a hedge. She made a right turn at Coast Highway. She could take a shortcut down the alley, but she preferred to walk past the front of the shops.

She unlocked the door to the Wedding Belles Bridal Salon, and the bell jingled cheerfully as she stepped inside. Her heels sank into the plush cream-colored carpeting as she walked to the office to put her purse and jacket away. She pulled up her schedule on the computer. It would be a quiet, easy day, with just one appointment at eleven. Shortly before ten, she turned the sign on the front door to OPEN.

She went to the workroom, her sanctuary, which Darlene pretty much allowed her to set up the way she wanted it. In this room, surrounded by beautiful fabrics and dresses, she was miles away from the real world and whatever problems were out there. She pulled her latest creation off the rack. Jennifer Burns was her eleven o'clock appointment, coming in for her final fitting. Max sat in on all the consultations, and Darlene used most of her ideas for the design and the fabrics. And, of course, Max did the pattern making and sewing. And yet, Darlene took most of the credit for it, as always.

She heard the front door jingle and a familiar voice called out her name. She felt butterflies in her stomach.

"I'm back here," she called to him.

"Hey, Max," the young man said, coming to the doorway. Andy Fuller wore a white shirt and pants, and his sandy brown hair fell loosely over his forehead.

"How's it going, Andy?" she asked, trying to sound casual, ignoring the way her heart beat a little faster.

"Oh, you know. Up to my elbows in flour since six. How 'bout you?"

"Just getting started. Jennifer's coming in for her final fitting at eleven." She scowled at the dress. "I'm so glad to be done with this gown. She's made so many changes I can't even keep up. This is her third wedding. Wouldn't you think she'd have it figured out by now?"

"Yeah, everyone will be glad when the wedding's over. I'm working on new cake samples for her. She was going to go with chocolate. Now she wants something different. I charge her every time, so I don't mind." He always looked at the bright side. "I almost forgot why I stopped by. How about having dinner with Stacy and me at the Crazy Fox tonight? It would be nice to catch up."

"I'd love to," Max said. She'd hardly seen Andy at all since he came back from college with his new bride a few weeks ago. She knew it was childish to avoid him, but she couldn't help herself. "I close at six. I can be there a little after that."

"Great! See you there!" He gave her a hug and left.

She felt ready to have Andy back in her life. Besides, if she kept avoiding him, he might think she still had a thing for him.

Andy had taken a few years off from school before he decided he wanted to be a doctor. Before he left for school, Max decided to finally admit to him she was in love with him. She invited him to her apartment and made him dinner. She drank a little too much wine, trying to get up the courage to say what she felt she needed to tell him. Why she always thought he felt the same way, she didn't know. But he didn't. He explained he loved her like a sister but nothing more. He tried to be kind, but she felt as if a little piece of her heart broke off that night and would always belong to Andy. She didn't know if she would ever get it back and feel whole again.

Telling herself to get back to work, she took Jennifer's dress to the fitting room, removed it from its plastic, and fluffed it out. Most brides would go for something simple for their third wedding, but not Jennifer. She spared no expense on her custom gown. Max went over every inch of the dress for the third time, searching for stray threads or any other imperfection.

While she waited, she decided to get started on one of the dresses she needed to alter. She got out her seam ripper and started taking out stitches. This was the least favorite part of her job. When the door jingled, she glanced up at the clock. 11:25. That woman was never on time. She just wanted to get this over with.

She went into the showroom and Jennifer Burns threw her designer purse on the sofa. Her blonde, highlighted hair was pulled back into a French twist, and her ivory cashmere sweater hugged her surgically enhanced curves. Her black thigh-high boots probably cost more than Max's first car. She always carried an expensive bottle of water in one hand and her phone in the other.

Without taking her eyes from her phone, Jennifer huffed, "I don't know why we couldn't have done the last fitting at my home."

"I didn't want to take the chance of anything happening to your gown," Max said. Jennifer had a lot of nerve expecting her to make house calls.

"I thought that was what plastic was for." Jennifer took a moment away from her phone to give Max a condescending glance.

"I like to be extra careful."

"Whatever."

Max led the bride-to-be into the fitting room and helped her into the gown. Jennifer put her phone down briefly to get into the dress and then picked it back up. Once Jennifer stood on the raised platform in the room Max called the Dream Room, she was a vision in a mermaid style gown of silk, tulle, and vintage lace.

Max held her breath. The dress was perfect, her most lovely creation yet. The only thing she didn't like were the sleeves Jennifer insisted on adding to hide her 38-year-old arms. It took a lot of ingenuity for Max to add sleeves to a strapless gown, but they looked as if they were a part of the original design. Jennifer took pictures of herself in the mirror with her phone.

"It's beautiful," Jennifer said, and Max let the air out of her lungs.

"I'm so glad you love it."

"But the sleeves have got to go." She turned around to admire herself from all angles.

Max couldn't speak for a moment. "But you asked us to add the sleeves."

"Oh, I know. But I've been working out with a new trainer, and my arms are in fabulous shape. I want to show them off. Besides, I think the dress looked better without them."

Max sighed. That's what she'd said in the first place. "Well, the wedding isn't for two weeks, so I have some time."

"Oh no," Jennifer replied. "I'm having pictures done tomorrow. I'll need it done by tonight."

Max said nothing, only stared at the other woman. She wanted to glare at her, but she was too polite. So much for her easy day.

"Of course, I'll pay you extra. Does $100 sound fair?" Her attention was back on her phone again, no doubt checking out the pictures of herself in her wedding gown.

"$200," Max answered firmly.

"Done. I'll be back at eight."

Darn. She should have charged more!

Max made a pot of Darjeeling tea in her imported English teapot. The idea of taking all those tiny white stitches out of the white lace dress made her shoulders tense up. She took a deep breath. She thought it would take a couple of hours to remove the sleeves from the dress. Then she needed to redo the top of the dress so there would be a clean line without the sleeves.

She called her friend Olivia and left her a message canceling their lunch plans. Olivia was the resident stage manager for the Crystal Shores Playhouse, and they had become friends when Max had helped out with the costumes for last summer's Shakespeare festival.

Getting out her trusty seam ripper, Max got to

work. After half an hour of painstakingly taking out nearly invisible stitches from white silk and lace, her head throbbed, and her stomach grumbled. The jingling of the door was a welcome interruption.

"Hi Max, it's me," Olivia called out.

Max went into the showroom and gave Olivia a hug. She never understood how Olivia always appeared so perfect and pulled together. Today she was wearing a crisp white shirt, pale blue linen slacks, and tan sandals. She would make a perfect Snow White with her pale complexion and long dark hair pulled back into a ponytail. In fact, she played the part for a children's show the theater put on last month.

"What are you doing here?" Max asked. "Didn't you get my message? I can't go to lunch today."

"But you still have to eat. I brought avocado sandwiches from Sprouts Cafe."

"Sounds healthy," Max said unenthusiastically.

"I knew you were going to say that, so I brought you a brownie for dessert."

"Yay!" Max clapped her hands. "Chocolate!"

Max took Olivia back to the workroom and covered the table with paper so they could eat.

"What's the big emergency that means you can't eat lunch?" Olivia asked as she took the sandwiches out of the bag and handed one to Max.

"It's Jennifer Burns." Max unwrapped the paper around her sandwich.

"Oh! That woman!"

"I thought you two were friends."

"Our friendship is being sorely tested. She's threatening to shut down the theater," Olivia said. "It's been there since the Twenties, and she wants to tear it down and build a strip mall."

"Jennifer owns the theater? Since when?"

"She got it in the divorce settlement when she and William Chase split up. It had been in the Chase family for years, but William inherited the land and the building a few years ago when his father passed away. Jennifer must have had an excellent attorney because she got the house and the theater."

"But doesn't the theater have a long-term lease?" Max took a big bite of her sandwich, which, as it turned out, tasted delicious. She might want to give this eating healthy thing a shot if it tasted this good.

"Our lease is up in June. The Chase family was always fair with us. They were supporters of the arts and the community. Jennifer doesn't seem to have the same priorities, and I've been trying to get her to see things our way." Olivia nibbled at her sandwich daintily. "Everyone is a wreck at the theater. It's not only that we'll lose our jobs. The theater means something to us. It means something to the community. It's an institution. We were all talking the other night about how she needs to be stopped."

"Anything you can do?"

"We haven't come up with anything yet, but we're working on it."

"She is a challenge, I'll say that." Max liked the word "challenge." It sounded nicer than pain in the you-know-what. "Anyway, once I get the sleeves off her dress, I'll be done with her."

"Let's not talk about her anymore." They ate in silence for a few minutes. "How's everything else going?"

Max had been so annoyed about Jennifer, that she'd almost forgotten her big news. "I've got something to tell you." Max waited until she was sure she had Olivia's full attention. "I got a call from my old boss at Bissette. They offered me the job."

"The assistant designer position?" Olivia reached over to grab her friend's hand and squeezed it. "I'm so happy for you!" Then her smile faded slightly. "I'm going to miss you," she said softly.

"I'll miss you too." She and Olivia had become close during the past several months. She didn't want to think about how much she would miss her. But they could talk on the phone whenever they wanted. And she would come home to visit. Max took the paper sandwich wrappers and threw them in the trash.

She heard the door jingle and went into the front room to see who had entered. Olivia followed her. River, the mailman, gave them both a big smile. It was hard to tell how old River was, and she certainly would never ask. He had a face weathered from the sun, and his thinning hair was pulled back into a ponytail.

"Hi, River. The waves looked big today."

"Too gnarly for me. There's a hurricane off the coast of Baja. Did you go for a walk on the beach this morning?"

"Yes, and it was lovely. I don't know why, but the loud, crashing waves are very calming to me. Of course, all the calm went out the window as soon as I got to work."

"That's not like you, Max," River said. "You usually go with the flow."

"I'm used to stressed out brides," Max said. "But some brides..." She didn't finish the thought. Why did she let that woman get to her?

"The Dalai Lama once said, 'I defeat my enemies when I make them my friends.'"

Max put her hands on her hips. "Really, River? I don't see that happening."

"Maybe Nietzsche is more appropriate for this occasion. He said, 'Be careful when you fight the monsters, lest you become one.'"

Max laughed. "Okay, River. I'll be careful."

River handed her a stack of mail, said "Namaste," and left.

"Time for brownies now?" Max asked Olivia.

Olivia laughed and Max followed her back to the workroom. She pulled a huge chocolate brownie out of the bag.

"Where's yours?" Max asked. "Or are we splitting this one?" Max hoped they weren't.

"No brownie for me," Olivia told her. "I feel so much better when I stay away from sugar. I'll let you get back to work."

Max sighed. She didn't want to get back to work yet. "Well, thanks for the lunch and making me take a break. I needed it."

After Olivia left, Max stared at the brownie. The age-old dilemma. Eat it now or save it for later. She stared at it for several seconds, then cut it in two pieces and ate one of the halves, saving the other half for later. She didn't know what Olivia was thinking. Chocolate made everything better.

Max went back to work taking out all the stitches and was only interrupted three times. One bride stopped in without an appointment and had no idea about what she wanted in a wedding dress. Max explained that she was only available by appointment this week and suggested diplomatically that she spend some time looking through magazines and come back with pictures of gowns that she liked. Another bride whose dress was on order came in to try on tiaras and veils, and one mother of the bride stopped in to ask for advice about a dress to wear at her daughter's wedding. Finally, when she was able to get back to Jennifer's dress, all that remained was to re-sew the seams and remove all evidence that sleeves ever existed. The rest of the sewing needed to be done by hand, which would take forever. It was her job, so she knew she had no reason to complain. That didn't mean she couldn't be crabby about it. She hoped there wouldn't be any more interruptions.

When she made the final stitch in the gown, she checked the time. It was five minutes to six. Yes! She quickly ran the vacuum cleaner over the carpet, closed up the shop and walked down the street to meet Andy and Stacy.

CHAPTER 2

*M*ax walked through the front door of the Crazy Fox and into the dark, wood-paneled interior. It took a moment for her eyes to adjust, and then she headed for the bar, waving hello to Burt, her favorite bartender. All the tables were already taken, and the room was full of lively conversations. Andy was waiting for her at a small table with two glasses of white wine. She felt a smile take over her face. Maybe they could be friends like they used to be if she could get past the awkwardness.

"Are both of these for me? I could use them." She sat down across from him.

Andy laughed and pushed one towards her. "Bad day?"

"Just a marathon with the seam ripper. Where's Stacy?" They were at a table for two. He was wearing a blue polo shirt that almost matched the color of his eyes. His hair was rumpled, as usual. Why did he have to look so boyishly handsome?

"Still at the bakery. Jennifer's stopping by to taste the latest cake samples I made. I told her I'd stay, but she told me to come have dinner with you."

"You left Stacy to deal with Jennifer alone?" Max took a sip of her wine. "Why would you do a thing like that?"

"Was that a bad idea?"

Max laughed. "I'm sure she'll be fine. I have a feeling Stacy can handle her, but I'm sorry she couldn't make it."

"I was kinda hoping you two would get to be friends. It'd be cool if my oldest friend and my wife got along."

"Hey, I'm not that old!"

Andy laughed. "You know what I mean."

"Tell you what. I'll invite her to dinner. Just the two of us. We can get to know each other a little better."

Andy's grin lit up his face. "That would be awesome." She loved the way the corners of his eyes crinkled when he smiled.

"I'm glad she doesn't mind us hanging out together." She assumed Andy never told Stacy what had happened. If he had, she doubted Stacy would have sent him to have dinner with her alone.

"Yeah, well, I told her how we used to play with worms together in the back yard when we were little. She knows you're like a sister to me."

"Don't forget the time you put a worm down my shirt. I still haven't forgiven you for that." Maybe once she moved back to New York it would be easier. At least she wouldn't have to see them so often. Andy had met Stacy when he went back to college to become a doctor. When he earned his B.S., he brought her home with him and married her. Andy had never told her why he didn't go on to med school, and he didn't seem to want to talk about it.

Andy called the waitress over and ordered sliders and onion strings for both of them. Max remembered the stone she had found on the beach and pulled it out of her pocket.

"Check it out. What do you think it is?" She held her hand out with the stone in her palm.

"It might be a gemstone of some kind," Andy offered. "You should take it to Amir's and ask them what it is. It could be valuable." He picked up the stone from her, touching her hand when he did. "It's funny how you're always finding things."

While they ate their sliders, she listened to Andy tell her about married life and the plans he and Stacy were making. It was the first time since he'd been back in town that they'd really had a long talk, and it was easier than she had expected. He told her that his parents planned to travel more now that he was home, and he and Stacy would take over the bakery in a couple of years so they could retire.

Andy pushed his empty plate away. "So, what's new with you?"

"I was offered a job with Bissette," she said.

"What? I didn't even know you were thinking of changing jobs." He finished the last gulp of his wine. "I didn't think you liked being a pattern maker that much. Though I know you loved living in New York."

"It's not my old job. It's an assistant designer position. It's a great opportunity. If things go well, I can move up to a designer position in a few years."

"That's great. I'm happy for you." His voice was flat.

"You don't sound happy," she said.

"I'm happy for you, but I'm gonna miss you. I like it with us both living in the same town again. I can pop by anytime." But he hardly ever did. He was too busy with his new wife and the bakery. Andy checked his watch. "It's almost eight. I better get going."

She had to get back to her shop to meet with Jennifer, so they said their goodbyes. It was a good feeling, being friends with him again. Maybe she'd meet someone in New York, someone who would make her forget all about Andy. Her track record with other men in Crystals Shores hadn't been much better. She was ready for a new start.

Back at the shop, Max put on her sewing apron. She always wore it for fittings because it had lots of pockets for a tape measure, pins, and other tools of the trade. The door jingled at eight o'clock prompt. Was Jennifer actually on time for once? She went to the showroom to greet Jennifer, but instead Stacy was standing there with a pink cake box in her hands.

"Hi, Max." Stacy greeted her cheerfully in her Texas drawl, putting the box down on the coffee table. "Is Jennifer here?"

Max gave her a hug. "No, but then she's always late. I missed you at dinner. I hope we can do it another time, maybe just the two of us. We'll let Andy work late while we trade stories."

"That'd be great!" Stacy's big brown eyes were eager like a puppy's. "I'd love to hear all about what Andy was like when he was a child. He says y'all played together."

"Yeah, our parents were friends. We've known each other for twenty years, since I was six and he was seven. When you're young, one year's age difference seems like a lot. I think he thought I was an annoying little kid. But he put up with me." She gestured to the coffee table. "What's up with the box?"

"I waited around for an hour, and Jennifer just now calls me and says to meet her here. I missed dinner for nothin'. I'd call her a word that rhymes with 'witch,' but I'm too much of a lady."

"Stacy! I've never heard you talk like that."

"Doggone it, that woman could make a preacher cuss. She changes her mind every time she turns around. She says she doesn't want chocolate, so we had to come up with somethin' different." Stacy opened the box and pointed to each square of cake. "Andy made carrot cake with cream cheese frosting, orange-ginger, lemon, almond with amaretto buttercream frosting, and this here's my latest creation, pecan pie cake."

"Wow! They look scrumptious. So, Jennifer's making last minute changes? How unlike her."

"Really?" Stacy appeared confused. "She musta changed her mind at least three times about what she wants. I wish she'd picked another baker."

Max made a mental note to skip sarcasm when it came to Stacy. "Well, I spent most of the day taking the sleeves off her dress. That was after she had me add them. Do you know how hard it is to add sleeves to a strapless gown? Luckily, it wasn't quite as difficult to remove them."

"Oh, she did it to you too? I don't know why I let her get under my skin. Do you know that Andy dated that...that..." Stacy tried to come up with the right word and finally settled for "...woman?"

"Yeah, I know. It's one of his few lapses of judgment."

"And she doesn't miss a chance to bring it up. Andy says they went out once, but the way she talks, you'd think they went steady. She talks like she knows him better'n me. I can't believe he dated her. I thought he had better taste."

"She's a beautiful woman, Stacy. And men are weak, at least when it comes to women. But he only has eyes for one beautiful woman now."

Stacy shot her a worried glance. "Who?"

Max just shook her head.

"Oh." Stacy smiled. "You mean me." She giggled.

"Good, I made you smile. Why don't you leave the cake with me, and I'll let you know which one she likes. Go home to your husband."

Before Stacy had a chance to get away, Jennifer entered. She threw her purse on the sofa. As usual, she had a bottle of water in one hand and her phone in the other.

"Hi, Jennifer," Max greeted her.

"I don't have much time. I'm meeting Chad at 8:30. His band plays at 9:00, and I still need to go over some details with him about the wedding. Why do grooms think all they have to do is show up to the wedding?"

Jennifer didn't wait for her to answer. She turned to Stacy. "Are those the cake samples?"

"Yes'm," Stacy answered. She opened the box and described each of the samples.

"You can go," Jennifer announced.

Stacy seemed annoyed for a moment, and then realized she didn't have to spend any more time in Jennifer's company. She exited out the front door with a quick "Bye!"

Jennifer made Max wait while she checked her phone. Finally, she opened the box and took a nibble out of one of the pieces.

"Interesting. I'll say one thing about that girl, she can bake."

"Actually, Andy made them. Stacy made the pecan pie cake. She's still learning the ropes."

Jennifer gobbled down several bites of cake.

"The almond is interesting. What's in the frosting?"

"I think Stacy said it was Amaretto."

She took a few more bites and seemed to be thinking it over. "Tell Stacy we'll go with the orange."

Max almost said she could tell her herself but decided not to. It was a wonder she didn't have a sore tongue with all the times she bit it when dealing with Jennifer.

They went back to the fitting room, and Max helped Jennifer into the gown. The bride-to-be stood on the pedestal with the mirrors reflecting back six perfect versions of Jennifer in the now strapless and even more stunning gown. Max's heart warmed as she viewed her creation.

"I don't know what Andy sees in that white trash of a wife he has."

And the spell was broken.

"Cinch up the bodice more," Jennifer demanded.

Max tightened the lacing on the back of the dress. She may have given it an extra tug for good measure.

"How's that?" she asked.

"That's good. I'm having a little trouble breathing, but that's okay, I'll get used to it."

"Are you sure? You're a little pale."

Jennifer chugged down the rest of her water and handed Max the empty bottle.

"Now you're a bit flushed. Are you okay?"

"I'm fine," Jennifer snapped. She twirled around on the pedestal and nearly lost her balance. Her eyes seemed unfocused.

"Would you like me to loosen the bodice?" Max asked.

"Just get me some more water," Jennifer demanded in a hoarse voice.

Max went into the office to get a bottle of water out of the mini fridge, but there weren't any left. She went into the storeroom where she knew there were extras. Before facing Jennifer again, she took a couple of deep breaths. What had River said about monsters? White trash! She had some nerve.

"I wish she would drop dead," she muttered under her breath. As she turned to go back into the Dream Room, she heard a thud and ran to see what had happened. Jennifer was lying on the floor, looking innocent and sweet in silk and white lace.

CHAPTER 3

$\mathcal{M}$ax's adrenaline kicked into overdrive. She flew over to Jennifer's side and checked for a pulse. It was weak, but at least her heart was still beating. She saw Jennifer's phone lying on the floor, picked it up and dialed 911. She wished she'd taken the CPR class at the community center they offered last summer.

"Don't panic. Don't panic," she told herself.

The operator kept her on the phone and asked her one question after another. Jennifer had a pulse and was breathing, albeit shallowly, so there was no need for CPR. She loosened the bodice so Jennifer could breathe more easily. Had she tightened it too much? The operator said they were sending an ambulance and kept her talking on the phone. What was taking them so long?

Sirens wailed in the distance, and Max ran to the front door. A fiftyish woman in a navy velour tracksuit with short spiky brown hair and cat-eye glasses dashed in and asked where the woman was who had fainted. Max was confused but motioned to the other room. Then she noticed the woman had a camera.

"Hey! What are you doing?" The woman was snapping photos of Jennifer. The sirens stopped in front of the shop.

Someone called out from the showroom. The paramedics rushed in and took over, checking Jennifer's vital signs. Where had the woman with the camera gone? She must have slipped out as soon as the ambulance had arrived.

Max stood by helplessly, not knowing what to do while they put an oxygen mask on Jennifer. Then they put Jennifer on a gurney and took her out the front door to the ambulance. Max gave Jennifer's purse to a female EMT.

"She's stabilized but still unconscious. We're taking her to Coast Memorial Hospital," the EMT told her. "Do you have contact information for her family?"

Max hesitated. She'd never met any of Jennifer's family. "I'll call her fiancé," she told the EMT.

"Do you have his name and number?" Max went back into the Dream Room to retrieve Jennifer's phone and looked up Chad's number for them. The EMTs had left when she realized she should have given them Jennifer's phone. She looked under the contacts for "Mom" or "Dad," but there were no entries.

Max dialed Chad's number. It went to voicemail, so she left him a message. Think! Jennifer was going to meet him at 8:30. His band was playing at 9:00, so she must have been meeting him at the Crazy Fox. She called the restaurant, but the line was busy. She called again, and it went to voicemail. What a way to run a restaurant, she thought.

She took off her apron, grabbed her purse, and locked up the shop. Then she remembered she didn't have a car. She could walk the four blocks home and get her dad's car or go straight to the restaurant. The latter choice was quicker.

She hurried down the street and waited impatiently for a break in traffic so she could cross Coast Highway. Once inside the restaurant, she headed for the bar area and peered around in the dim light. She spotted Burt behind the bar.

"Have you seen Chad?" she asked.

"Hi, Max," he answered. "Is everything all right?"

"No, it's definitely not all right. I need Chad."

"He's at the last booth in the back."

Chad sat with his back to her, his sun-lightened, dirty blonde hair flowing in waves down to his shoulders. She hurried over to him and interrupted his conversation to tell him Jennifer had been taken to the hospital.

He jumped up, knocking over his beer. "What happened?"

"I don't know. She was trying on her wedding dress, and she collapsed. The paramedics came."

"Is she going to be all right?"

"They said she was stabilized. I don't know anything else."

"What hospital did they take her to?" he asked.

"Coast Memorial." Obviously, Chad hadn't lived in

27

town long enough to know there was just one hospital.

"Where is it? Can you take me there?"

"I don't have a car."

"I'll drive. You show me the way." He reached in his pants pockets for his keys and headed for the back door. "What happened?" he asked again.

Max told him everything she could remember, which wasn't much. His Mercedes was parked behind the restaurant, and they climbed in.

Chad raced to the hospital while Max clutched the armrest. Max asked if he had her family's phone numbers.

"Her only family is her mother." When Max told him she didn't find a number on Jennifer's phone for "Mom," he told her they were not on the best of terms and had deleted her number from her phone after their last fight. He handed her his phone and told her to call Sonia. Max told Sonia her daughter was unconscious, and she had been taken to the hospital. Max continued to give directions to Chad while she told Sonia what little she knew. She hung up just as he pulled up in front of the emergency room door, jumped out, and rushed inside.

"You can't park there," a man in scrubs yelled after him. He turned to Max. "Move it."

"But it's not my car," Max said.

"I don't care. Move it."

Max stared at the Mercedes. Chad had left the keys in it, so she got in the driver's seat and started it up. The engine growled. She very slowly drove it to the parking lot and pulled into a spot.

Max stepped through the doors of the emergency room. This was the first time she'd been at the hospital since her mother passed away. She blinked back tears that welled up suddenly and looked for Chad, but he was nowhere to be found. She went up to the window and asked the nurse if they had any information about Jennifer. They asked her relationship to Jennifer and then said they couldn't release any information. She asked if Chad was there, and they directed her to a waiting room down the hall. Chad was inside, pacing back and forth in the small room.

"She's going to be okay, right?" he asked her. She didn't know what to say. "Maybe she passed out from low blood sugar or something. She gets lightheaded if she doesn't eat."

"Yeah, maybe that's what happened."

"I always told her to make sure and eat. She was always skipping meals or eating next to nothing."

"Is there someone I can call to come be with you?" Max asked.

"I don't really have anyone except Jennifer."

Max decided to keep him company until they let him see Jennifer. They waited in silence while Max watched the minutes tick by on the wall clock. Finally, the door opened, and a doctor entered. Max and Chad jumped to their feet.

"I'm Doctor Meyer," he told them. "Are you relatives of Jennifer Burns?"

"I'm her fiancé, Chad Stevenson," Chad told him.

The doctor turned to Max.

"She collapsed in my shop," she explained.

"I see." Turning back to Chad, the doctor said, "Her mother is with her now. I'm sorry to have to tell you this, but Ms. Burns didn't make it."

Chad's mouth hung open slightly and he said nothing for several seconds, just staring at the doctor.

"No!" he shouted. "It can't be! We're getting married! She can't die!"

Chad seemed angry, and Max was surprised when he started to weep.

"I love her," he sobbed. "She can't be gone!"

Max tried to console the musician she barely knew while she tried to make sense of what had happened. She reached over to pat his arm, and he grabbed her and started sobbing on her shoulder. This is uncomfortable, she thought, as she imagined his tears seeping through her favorite sweater. Then she felt bad worrying about her clothes when someone was dead. Maybe she was in shock.

"There, there," she said, not knowing what else to say. How did someone in seemingly perfect health die so suddenly? It didn't make sense.

Max glanced at the doctor who appeared impatient. Chad composed himself and turned to ask the doctor what had happened. The doctor's expression turned to one of empathy.

"Can I see her?" Chad asked.

"I'll take you to her," the doctor answered. "Wait here," he told Max.

She stayed in her chair obediently. She checked her sweater to see if Chad had gotten any mascara on it besides the tears. Hey, he was a rock musician. She inspected her sweater, and not only was there no mascara, but it wasn't moist at all. Not even a little.

Max reached in her purse to call her dad. As she searched for her phone, she thought she should call Olivia too, but her phone wasn't in her purse. She must have left it at the shop in her rush. They must have payphones, although she couldn't remember the last time she'd seen one. She went to the nursing station and was directed to a payphone near the main entrance. She found a quarter at the bottom of her purse and dialed her dad's number. He didn't answer, so she left him a message to come pick her up at the hospital. She didn't remember Olivia's number, or anyone else's. She felt lost without her phone.

She went back to the waiting room and waited impatiently. This couldn't be happening. She flipped through magazines, not reading the words on the pages. If someone as young and healthy as Jennifer could die, then anyone could. She wished her dad would get there. After an hour, when Chad hadn't reappeared and her dad hadn't arrived to rescue her, she started to search in the bottom of her purse for more change so she could call a cab. Just then, the door opened. She expected to see Chad or her father, but instead it was a tall, dark-haired man in a neatly tailored, navy blue suit.

"Are you Max?" he asked.

"Yes," she answered, standing up. "Max Walters."

"I'm detective Jason Cruz of the Crystal Shores Police Department."

He asked her for the address of the shop and the

name of the landlords. He got on the phone, stepping into the hall before she was able to hear any of his conversation.

After a few minutes, he returned. "I have some questions if you have a few moments." He motioned for her to sit back down and took the chair next to her. He took a small device out of his pocket. "I'm going to record this conversation. Is that acceptable to you?"

Max nodded. Since when were policemen this handsome?

"The whole recording thing works better if you actually speak." His green eyes gazed into hers.

"Oh. Yes. I mean it's fine with me. If you record it." Cruz was a Spanish surname, wasn't it? How interesting that he had green eyes.

"I understand that Ms. Burns collapsed in your shop."

"What? I mean, yes. She went thud. Right in my shop. I went in the back room for just a minute, and when I came back, there she was on the floor."

"What was your relationship to the deceased?"

"I made her wedding gown."

"I see. Most of the shops aren't open evenings. Do you typically stay open late?"

"No. We usually close at six. She had an appointment. I was putting the final touches on her wedding gown because she needed it for pictures tomorrow."

"Did she eat or drink anything while she was at your shop?"

Max told him about the cake samples and the water Jennifer had been drinking.

"It was London water, I think. I'm pretty sure that was the brand. She always had it with her. Do they know why she died? Did she have some sort of allergic reaction?" If that was the case, why would the police be questioning her? Her death must at least have been suspicious. "Do you think she was poisoned?"

"Poisoned?" He seemed taken aback, and then quickly regained his composure. "It would be premature to discuss cause of death at this time," he said, sounding very diplomatic.

"She was young and healthy. She shouldn't be dead." She tried to fight back the tears, but she was losing the battle.

"Are you all right?" he asked.

"No. No, I'm not. The last time I was at this hospital was when my mother died." She got a crumpled tissue out of her purse and dabbed at her eyes. "Can I go home now?"

"Are you okay to drive?"

"I don't have a car. I came with Chad."

"Would you like a ride? I'm on my way to the shop next."

"That would be really nice of you." She smiled at him, looking into his eyes. Was she flirting? This was not the right time or place for that. She looked down at the floor and said, "But you don't need to bother. I can get a cab."

Before he could insist as she was hoping he would, her dad walked in the room. She threw herself into his arms. Everything was going to be okay now that he was here.

She introduced the detective to her father and asked if he had any more questions.

"They can wait," Detective Cruz said. "I'll need your number so I can call you and let you know when you can go back into your shop."

"What? I can't go into my shop?" It took her a moment to realize why. "Oh, it's a crime scene."

"Hold on. We don't know if a crime has been committed. Anyway, we should be done by tomorrow."

She was about to leave when she remembered something. "There was a woman who arrived just before the ambulance and was taking pictures."

"Spiky brown hair and glasses?" Detective Cruz asked. Max nodded. "I've run into her before. I'll call you tomorrow, but if you need me, here's my card."

Max took his card and said goodbye. She walked out of the hospital with her dad, unable to shake the idea that Jennifer had been poisoned. But if so, who had done it?

"What the heck happened tonight?" Richard asked as they climbed into his red and white Mini Cooper.

"Jennifer Burns collapsed at the shop and died at the hospital."

"Jennifer Burns, the real estate agent? Weren't you making her wedding dress?"

"Yes, that's why she was at my shop tonight." She told him about picking up Chad and going with him to the hospital.

"How did she die? She seemed to be in perfect health."

"She was. I'm pretty sure the police think she might

34

have been poisoned." The car pulled up in front of the house and her dad parked the Mini in a minuscule parking spot between two SUVs. They stepped through the wooden gate into the front patio. The rose bushes were getting out of control. She hadn't noticed because she always came in the back door. She'd have to volunteer to do some pruning. Her mom had always taken care of the gardening. Her mom had taken care of so many things, especially Max and her dad. Richard pulled open the heavy oak front door and they stepped into the living room.

Max sat down on the sofa, and her dad offered her hot chocolate.

"Don't you have anything stronger?" she asked. "It's been a rough day. I can hardly see straight after taking out all those stitches. Do you know how hard it is to remove hundreds of tiny white stitches out of white fabric?"

"And there was the woman who dropped dead in your shop," Richard offered, and poured his daughter a large glass of cognac.

"Yes, I hadn't forgotten. In spite of the fact that she could be difficult, to say the least, she didn't deserve to die. But if she was poisoned, I bet the suspect list is going to be a mile long." She took a sip of the cognac. "Thanks, Dad. I needed this. And thanks for coming to pick me up." She wanted to say more, like how she felt safe having him there.

"This is like *Killer Cupcakes* that we read last year. Do you remember? There was poison in the cupcakes."

"Well, I hope it's not like that book. Stacy brought

over cake samples tonight for Jennifer to try. I'm sure they'll take the cake box to test for poison. Andy's the one who made the cake. Except for the pecan pie cake. Stacy made that one. Anyway, once they test the cake, they'll know there was no poison in it."

"I hope you're right. Did the detective say how long it would take?"

"No, but I would think they'd know by tomorrow, wouldn't you think?"

"I suppose so." Her dad seemed thoughtful. "Speaking of the detective, I saw the way he was looking at you. He'll definitely be questioning you more."

"Dad, really. He *is* questioning me again. Tomorrow. After all, she was there when she collapsed."

"Okay, whatever you say, Max." He brought over the bottle to top off her glass, but she shook her head. The last thing she needed was a hangover tomorrow.

"I'm worried about Stacy and Andy. What if there was something in the cupcakes that Jennifer had a reaction to? They'll feel responsible." She got up and took her glass to the kitchen. She didn't really think it was an allergic reaction. She thought it was poison. Was it her suspicious nature that made her think that Jennifer had been murdered? She didn't think she was naturally suspicious, just naturally curious.

"Just don't jump to the conclusion that she was murdered."

"Why would you say that?" It was like her dad could read her mind. She wasn't about to admit to him she was already making a list of suspects in her head.

"You're always solving mysteries. Everyone in town knows if they've lost something or have some suspicions about someone, you're the one to go to. I'm surprised that detective hasn't heard of you after you knew where to look for Joey Simpson when the police didn't."

"Dad, I found Joey because I'm observant. He loves trains, so it wasn't a big stretch to guess he'd be hiding under the train tracks."

"Maybe not. But no one else thought of it. I remember when you wanted to be a detective. You even went to school for it."

"I took one forensic science class and one criminal law class." The forensic science class was fascinating, but she didn't get a very good grade in her criminal law class. It was just too boring. That was when she decided to go to design school instead, since it was her other love. "That doesn't exactly make me an expert. Besides, I'm sure the police will figure things out. Now, I'm going to get some sleep. I'm exhausted." She got up and gave her dad a long hug. He gave her a kiss on the cheek and told her to sleep well.

She walked out the back door, across the courtyard, and up the stairs to her apartment. She got into her pajamas, and crawled into bed, but as tired as she was, she lay there wide awake. How does a perfectly healthy woman die suddenly? Her gut told her it wasn't an allergic reaction or some unknown health problem.

When she finally closed her eyes, she saw the face of the green-eyed detective. Hopefully, he hadn't noticed she was trying to flirt. How embarrassing.

CHAPTER 4

*W*hen Max awoke, it was just like any other day. Until she sat up in bed and remembered that it wasn't. She marveled at how normal everything seemed even though someone had just died.

The first thing she did was to call Darlene and leave her a message on her cell phone about what had happened. Since her boss was on a cruise ship, Max wasn't sure how long before she'd get the message, but Darlene was not going to be happy, Max knew that much for sure. Jennifer still owed over a thousand dollars for the dress. Should she wait for Darlene to take care of that when she got back, or would Darlene expect her to take care of it? It seemed insensitive to bring it up to Jennifer's mother or Chad at a time like this.

She didn't know how long until she'd be let into the shop, so she put on her sweats planning to head to the beach for a walk. The thick fog hung in the air just like yesterday, but yesterday Jennifer was alive and now she wasn't. She got to the end of the street and turned back around.

She entered her dad's house through the back door, and when she saw him, she gave him a long hug.

"You all right?" he asked.

"Yeah. Don't ever die, okay?" His smile warmed her heart. "In fifty years, you can die. Not a minute sooner."

"Good thing I take care of myself."

"I think you should switch to non-fat creamer for your coffee."

"I will if you will," he answered.

"Okay, we'll think about it, then." She spooned up a bowl of oatmeal and sat down at the table.

They talked about their plans for the day, the weather, Richard's upcoming gallery show—everything except Jennifer's death.

After breakfast, she took a long shower. She tried to think about the day ahead, but her mind kept going back to the moment she saw Jennifer lying on the floor. She put on the same black slacks she'd worn yesterday with a different sweater. Grabbing her leather jacket, she walked down the stairs and decided to hang out in her dad's kitchen until Detective Cruz called her. She got the call when she was on her third cup of coffee, which was two more than her usual.

By this time, the fog had lifted, and as she walked to work the familiar fluffy clouds floated by in the sky. Yesterday, she'd barely noticed them, but today she gazed at them and memorized their shapes. The birds chirped and twittered and flew in and out of the bushes.

She walked past the same houses, but this time, she noticed every detail. She tried to name all the types of flowers, but there were many she didn't know the names of. She recognized begonias, geraniums, and pansies. And there were roses of every color and size.

She unlocked the front door and felt comforted by the friendly jingle the door made. She checked her calendar and was relieved to see her only appointment was at two o'clock. Detective Dreamy, er, Cruz, was coming by to question her more. Hopefully, it would be quiet until then.

Looking around the showroom, she was aware that the cake box was gone, but everything else looked the same. She hung up her jacket, put her purse in the desk drawer and then hunted for her phone. She couldn't find it anywhere. She used the landline to call it, but she didn't hear it ring. She went in the workroom and picked up her sewing apron that she'd thrown on a chair the night before and found her phone in the pocket. Just like she figured, it was dead, so she put it on the charger in the office.

In spite of having drunk three cups of coffee, a cup of tea sounded nice and relaxing, but she couldn't find her teapot. The police must have taken it too. Teapots just didn't get up and walk away.

The door jingled and she found Stacy in the showroom. "You gotta tell me everything." She hadn't even bothered to take off her flour-covered apron. "The police came by this morning and asked me and Andy tons of questions all about Jennifer. They said she's dead. What in the bejeezus happened?"

"I don't know much more than you do," Max said. "She passed out while she was trying on her wedding dress and died at the hospital." Max didn't want to share her suspicion yet that Jennifer had been poisoned, especially to Stacy.

"They had us make a list of every ingredient that was in the cake samples we made for her. She never said nothin' about any allergies. I feel just awful. What if it was something we put in one of our cakes?"

"I'm sure it wasn't." Max tried to sound reassuring.

The local FedEx deliveryman, Curtis, came through the door with a package for Max. Stacy said she had to get back to the bakery.

"It's from Ireland," Curtis told her.

"What?" Max asked, her mind elsewhere.

"The package. It's from Ireland. Are you okay?"

"Yes, I'm just a little distracted. I've been waiting for this package for ages. It's handmade lace I ordered a month ago. Thanks." She looked at Curtis as if she'd just noticed he was there. "By the way, how's school going?"

"Great! I applied for an internship with a video game company, so you might get a new delivery person soon."

"Good for you! You better promise to come back to visit."

After Curtis left, Max went to the workroom to open the package, but was interrupted when the front door jingled again. So much for her quiet morning. She walked into the showroom and a young woman in jeans and a red sweater stood there. It really was sweater weather, she thought. In southern California, there are a limited number of days to wear sweaters, so when the thermometer dropped below 65 degrees, everyone puts on their sweaters. The woman was petite, African American, with curls that came down to her shoulders. She seemed so familiar, but Max couldn't remember how she knew her.

"Hi!" Max tried to sound cheerful. "I'm sorry, I don't remember your name."

The woman smiled. "You wouldn't. I'm pretty sure you never heard it. I'm Molly Harper. I'm one of the EMTs from last night."

"Oh, that's where I know you from," Max smiled back. "What brings you here today?"

"I didn't know if I needed an appointment. Do you have time?"

"Sure," Max answered, her curiosity piqued. "Have a seat." She gestured to the overstuffed armchairs. "Would you like some coffee or water?"

"No, nothing, thank you. I don't want to waste your time, so I'll get right to the point. I'm getting married in December. It may seem gruesome, but the dress the woman was wearing last night, well, it was breathtaking!"

"Thank you." Max smiled proudly. "It was one of our original designs."

"My mom told me you're a designer. She knows your dad from yoga class."

"Yeah, I don't need a PR agent as long as my dad's around."

"So, getting to the point, like I said, how much would a dress like that cost?"

"It depends on the design and the fabric choices. Jennifer had very expensive taste."

"I've set aside $5,000. I saved it up for a gown I saw in a magazine. Now it's discontinued. Of course, it wasn't as beautiful as the dress you made."

"We can do a custom-made gown within your budget," Max said. "Jennifer's was quite a bit more than that, but she insisted on the most expensive materials, and she made changes along the way that drove the cost up." So many changes. "Do you have a picture of the dress that you wanted?"

Molly pulled out a folded magazine page out of her purse and held it out. It was worn and creased. It was a fairly simple dress, nothing too difficult to recreate.

"Why don't we make an appointment and talk more about it?" Max suggested. "If you want, you can bring one or two people to help. I don't recommend more than that for the first consultation. I'll have you try on dresses so we can find the most flattering silhouette for you. I'll find one similar to this picture, and you can see if that's really what you want. I have sources for discontinued gowns, so I can't promise, but I might be able to find it for you."

"That sounds great!"

"It'll be fun. We'll put on some music and have a great time. After all, you only get married once. That's the plan, right? Who's the lucky man?"

Molly was marrying a man she had met in med school. They'd even talked about opening a joint practice after they began practicing medicine since they both planned to be pediatricians. Max thought she'd love to take her child to see Molly someday. She hoped she would have the chance.

Molly had a huge smile talking about her fiancé. Max's favorite thing about her business was seeing that smile. Then the smile faded.

"It's so sad your client was poisoned before she was able to wear your dress."

"You think she was poisoned? Did you talk to the doctor?"

"Maybe I shouldn't have said anything. I learned about cyanide poisoning in med school," Molly said. "Her skin was pink and there was a smell of almonds."

"She had just eaten cake my friends made. I hope they get the lab tests back soon, so they know it wasn't poisoned."

"It takes several days or more to get lab results. It's not like on TV."

After Molly left, Max thought about the cake and the water bottle. It had to be the water. She knew London water couldn't be healthy.

It was almost noon when the door jingled again, and Fiona McNulty entered. When Fiona's husband passed away a few years ago, she retired and opened The Knitpickers yarn shop next door with her sister Teresa. She wore a bedazzled baseball cap and an oversized t-shirt and leggings. Her sneakers were bright orange.

"How are you, dear?" Fiona asked with concern in her voice. She hugged Max tightly. A little too tightly.

"I'm fine," Max answered once Fiona let go. Obviously, Fiona knew. How long would it take before everyone knew? News traveled fast in this town. And once Fiona got the scoop, it spread like wildfire.

"I saw it in the *Daily Breeze* this morning. I can't believe you found the body. How awful for you."

Okay, everyone was going to know sooner than later if it was in the local paper. "I didn't actually find a body. Jennifer collapsed in the shop, and I called the paramedics. She died at the hospital."

"Still, how terrible for you."

"I just hope what happened doesn't chase away business. I just know somehow Darlene will blame me for it." Why was she thinking about business at a time like this? "It's awful for Jennifer and her family, or whoever actually loved her. You know, her parents and her fiancé."

"Oh yes, no doubt. I'm sure her mother is devastated. Her father passed away years ago. But I wouldn't worry about business. You'll probably be getting more calls than ever, even if most of them are just curious or looking for gossip. Anyway, Teresa and I just wanted you to know we're here if you need anything. She asked me to give you this." She handed Max a gift bag.

Max pulled something knitted out of the bag. Was it some kind of hideous hat? "Oh, that's nice."

"You have no idea what it is, do you?" Fiona chuckled.

Max shrugged sheepishly.

"It's a tea cozy," Fiona said. "You know how Teresa is. She knits scarves for Christmas presents and baby booties and blankets for new moms. I guess she figured having someone die in your shop warranted a tea cozy."

Max turned it over in her hands. "It's great! My tea always gets cold. Although, they took my teapot. I think they're testing it for poison."

"She was poisoned! How gruesome!"

"Actually, she looked quite beautiful laying on the floor of the Dream Room. Serene. And they say they're not sure how she died. But I'm pretty sure she was poisoned." She thought of Jennifer lying there and shivered.

"So, she didn't suffer."

"No, I don't think so."

"That's good. Though I suppose it will disappoint some people."

"Fiona!"

"Oh, you know me. Always saying out loud what other people only think. Does this mean we have a murderer in our midst?"

"I guess that's possible." It was a disturbing thought. It could be someone she knew. Maybe whoever gave Jennifer the bottle of water?

The door jingled again, and her friend Eric Mancini rushed in.

"I can't leave you alone for five minutes!" He grabbed her in one of his all-encompassing hugs, and whispered in her ear, "are you okay?"

"I've been better," Max admitted, although hugs did help.

Eric owned Flower to the People, the flower shop a block down the street. He was one of her best friends ever since he did her mother a favor and took Max to the prom when she didn't have a date. He was nearly thirty at the time, with gorgeous dark brown eyes and long eyelashes. For once in her life, other girls in school envied Max. He hadn't yet come out to everyone, so they didn't know he was gay. He confided in Max as they sat at an all-night diner. They talked until 3:00 A.M., drinking about a gallon of coffee, and were fast friends ever since.

Eric noticed Fiona standing there and they gave each other air kisses.

"I'll let you two talk," Fiona said, adding to Eric, "Isn't this exciting? I mean it's terrible, simply terrible, but exciting!"

"Yes, it's terrible. Jennifer was…"

"Yes, she was," Fiona said, and left.

"How are you?" Eric asked, holding her at arm's length as if to inspect her.

"I'm fine." Max didn't know quite how she felt, but she was alive and kicking, so she wasn't going to complain.

"Don't lie to me. You do not handle stress well, and we both know it. Turn around." He turned Max around and started to massage her shoulders. It felt wonderful. She was on edge this morning, which was no surprise. "You are wound up tight! Tell me everything."

Max suspected that getting the gossip was more

important to him than helping her relax. He finished rubbing her shoulders and the two sat down. Max told him everything that had happened since Jennifer came in yesterday morning for her fitting, including every detail.

"So, the detective is hot, huh?"

"Is that what you got out of the whole story?" she asked.

"I have my priorities straight. Speaking of straight, is he?"

The door jingled yet again, and there was Detective Cruz in a dark suit, white shirt and tie. She reminded herself not to stare.

"You can ask him yourself if you want," she whispered. She introduced the detective to Eric, who volunteered he went to school with Jennifer.

"Do you know if she had any enemies?" Detective Cruz asked.

"Now that is going to be a long list," Eric said. "Jilted ex-boyfriends, jealous girlfriends, and then there's everyone she pissed off with her demands for her wedding."

"Did you ever see her arguing with anyone?" the detective asked.

"She argued with everyone, especially all her vendors. I bet the only one she didn't argue with was Max, because Max doesn't argue with anyone."

"I don't argue with customers. Darlene says the customer's always right." Max said

Eric continued. "You just complain to me about them later. But that's what friends are for."

"Was there anyone in particular that she had problems with?" Detective Cruz asked.

"There were a few, actually," Eric said.

"If you wouldn't mind putting together a list for me, I'd appreciate it. I understand you were Jennifer's florist for the wedding. When was the last time you saw her?"

"Last week. I can check my calendar, but I'm pretty sure it was Wednesday. I'll get to work on that list for you," Eric said, and left abruptly, leaving her alone with the detective.

"Is there somewhere we can talk where we won't be interrupted?" Cruz asked.

"How about the office? Although I'm here by myself, so there may be interruptions." He gave her a look that made her feel like a third grader in trouble with the teacher. "I suppose I could lock the door and put the closed sign up."

"Thank you."

While she turned the sign around, the phone started to ring. She stared at it, wanting to answer but let it go to voicemail. She led him into the office and took a seat behind the desk. Detective Cruz seemed out of place in a flowered armchair.

"We couldn't find a London water bottle," he said, getting down to business. "My people searched the shop and went through all the dumpsters in the back."

"Maybe I was wrong. It might have been another brand." She didn't think she was wrong, though. She was known for being extremely observant.

"We retrieved several bottles, so we're testing them all. And the cake samples."

"You don't really think Andy or Stacy had anything to do with it? What possible motive could they have?"

"We have to follow every lead. Did you know that Mr. Fuller used to date Ms. Burns?"

"I'd heard they went out, but I think it was just once, a long time ago." What was he getting at? "I think she dated every eligible man in town. And maybe some not so eligible."

"Did Mrs. Fuller know they were still in contact?"

"Sure. Their bakery was making her wedding cake." She paused. "Oh, but that's not what you mean, is it? No way! Andy only has eyes for Stacy. Jennifer just liked to rub it in to Stacy that they used to date. But it was only one date."

"Uh huh. So did it bother Mrs. Fuller when Ms. Burns would rub it in?"

"You bet it did! She can be a little insecure, and she vented once about what Jennifer had said…." Suddenly, Max realized she was saying too much and shut up.

"Hmmm…"

He could be so frustrating! What did hmmm… mean?

"If being jealous of a gorgeous ex-model is a motive for murder, then you've got a long list of suspects." She heard the phone ringing again in the other room. She hated not answering the phone.

"Actually, it is a motive for murder. But I don't jump to conclusions. I let the evidence speak for itself. Do you have any additional information?"

She hesitated. Should she mention that Andy actually baked the cakes? Of course, she had to tell him the truth. If he were a good detective, he'd find the murderer, and she would help as much as she could. She told him Stacy only made the pecan pie cake, and then remembered something.

"I heard a lot of people were upset she was closing down the theater," she said. "Their lease is up in June, and she's planning to turn it into a shopping mall or something."

"Interesting." He stared right at her. She felt as if he were trying to see right through her. It made her very uneasy. "Anything else?"

"I can ask around."

"No!" he snapped, startling her. "I've heard about you getting involved in police business before, and you need to stay out of it. We're waiting for the toxicology reports, but we have every reason to believe that cause of death is cyanide poisoning, so that means there is a murderer out there. If you think of anything, call me, but don't go asking questions. I'm sorry," his voice softened. "It's my job to protect the people of this town, and the last thing I expected to find in Crystal Shores was a murderer. You grew up in this town, didn't you?" he asked.

"All my life, until I moved to New York about two years ago. Nothing exciting ever happens in this town, which I used to think was boring, but now I think boring isn't so terrible."

"What brought you back to Crystal Shores?"

"I came back a year ago when my mother was sick."

"I remember you said she passed away recently. I'm very sorry. It's never easy to lose a parent, but it's especially hard when they're young."

"My mom took care of everything. She took care of my dad and me. She was an engineer, so she was the practical one. She supported us in everything we did, let us be creative and follow our dreams. I feel completely lost without her."

He leaned forward in the flowered armchair and shook his head sadly. "I know the feeling."

"Did you lose a parent?" she looked at Detective Cruz, realizing there was more to him than just the brusque, efficient cop.

"My dad was a police detective. I always wanted to be like him, so I followed in his footsteps. He was just a month from retirement when he was killed in the line of duty."

He stood up. "Thank you for your time," he said, sounding again like the efficient detective.

She followed him to the front room and asked a few more questions about the murder, but he wouldn't give her any information. She wondered if he even had more information. He reminded her to call if she thought of anything else, then he walked out the door and presumably out of her life. Eric was right. He was hot, in a clean-shaven, buttoned-down kind of way. She liked her guys more average looking. A little rougher around the edges. A little more easygoing, and not so bossy.

Still, she would miss their little visits.

CHAPTER 5

*M*ax went back to the workroom and eagerly grabbed a pair of scissors to open the package from Ireland. She'd ordered the lace over a month ago and couldn't wait to see it. Then the door jingled. She sighed. Oh well, she'd waited this long.

"Max, it's me," her friend Olivia called out.

"I'm coming," she called back. She walked into the front room and gave her friend a hug.

"I just heard about Jennifer. I can't believe it. I just saw her last night. And now she's dead." Olivia blinked back tears.

"I'm so sorry, Olivia." She didn't think Olivia and Jennifer were that close, but now she wasn't sure. "I should have called you last night. I wasn't thinking. Or I was thinking too much, I'm not sure."

"You think you're going to live forever and then without a warning, you're gone."

"Olivia, are you okay?" Max asked. Olivia's eyes were red.

"Sorry. I came here to console you after having her drop dead right in your shop. It's just that she was so young. I've never known anyone who died so young."

"You came to console me? How sweet." Olivia was that kind of a person – always thinking of others.

"I can't imagine what it would be like to discover a dead body. It must have been simply awful for you!" As a theater person, Olivia was appropriately dramatic. It was one of the things Max loved about her.

"Well, she wasn't actually dead when I found her. She passed out after she tried on her wedding dress. She died at the hospital."

"Who are your suspects?" Olivia asked.

"My suspects? What are you talking about? They're not even sure about cause of death."

"The rumor is she was murdered. Don't tell me you're not putting together all the suspects and the clues. Remember how you wanted to be a detective?"

"That's just because of all the Agatha Christie books I read." Max still loved to read mysteries and she watched *The Big Sleep* at least once a year. Why didn't they make movies like that anymore? When she was a teenager, she secretly wanted to be Sam Spade.

"But you took all those criminology classes in college before you decided to go to design school."

"I took two classes. But I changed majors when I realized how hard the classes were."

"And boring," Olivia added.

"Well, criminal law was boring, that's true. But my forensic science class was fascinating."

"I heard she was poisoned."

"Boy, word gets around this town fast." Max leaned closer. "They think it's cyanide."

"You've talked to the police? Who do they think did it?"

"I don't know. The detective didn't tell me much. I know they're testing all the water bottles they found, and my teapot, and the cake samples Andy made. Stacy brought it over last night before we did the final fitting. Final. Gee, it sure was."

"They can't suspect Andy!" Olivia sounded shocked.

"I'm afraid they do since he made the cake. And maybe Stacy too."

"So, you'll have to investigate."

"What? No, this is serious. The police detective seems very capable. I'm sure he'll realize Andy and Stacy didn't have motives and cross them off his list. Kinda creepy that there might be a killer out there, isn't it?"

"Yeah, creepy."

Could the killer be someone they knew? The town of Crystal Shores was filled with nice, normal people. They were her neighbors, people she passed on the sidewalk and said hello to at the grocery store. It must have been an outsider who killed Jennifer. That's what she wanted to believe, but she knew murderers usually knew their victims. Which meant it was quite likely that Jennifer knew the murderer, and probably she did too.

The door jingled and Fiona's sister Teresa came in. She wore a flowing white embroidered tunic and loose tan slacks. Her silver hair fell in a braid down her back to her waist. Teresa greeted Olivia with a hug.

"I brought you a teapot to borrow." Teresa handed Max a flowered teapot. "Fiona said the police took yours. I know how much you love your tea."

"Thank you!" Max said. "That's so thoughtful of you. I hadn't even thought about what I was going to do without a teapot."

"Fiona says she was poisoned. How dreadful!" She added in a hushed voice, "Any idea who did it?"

"I was just telling Olivia they're testing my teapot and what was left of the cake."

"What cake?"

"Stacy brought over cake samples for Jennifer to taste last night. Andy made them. Except Stacy made a pecan pie cake. Doesn't that sound amazing?"

"That sounds delicious. Are they going to start selling it at the bakery?" Teresa asked.

"I don't know. If not, I'm sure we can get Stacy to make one for us. She really is sweet."

"That's certainly nice of you to say so, considering." Teresa patted Max on the shoulder. Max had told her when she was barely a teenager that she was going to marry Andy. Max always assumed they would end up together. It was naïve of her to assume Andy felt the same way, but for years she did.

"It must be hard for you," Olivia added.

"I'm fine," Max told both of them. She wished she'd

never told them how she felt about Andy, but they probably would have figured it out anyway.

Teresa frowned. "If Andy and Stacy made the cake samples, do the police suspect one of them of murdering Jennifer?"

"I don't know who they suspect at this point. The detective really wasn't in a sharing mood when he was here earlier."

"But you're going to figure out who the murderer is?" Teresa said it more like a statement than a question.

"What? No, the police will figure it out. Although I would like to know what evidence they have," Max said.

"Remember when you were a little girl, and your hamster went missing?" Teresa asked. "You questioned everyone. 'Where were you the night of' whatever night it was. You were adorable. I thought you were going to be a detective when you grew up."

"I wanted to be," Max admitted. "The other kids wanted to be princesses and space pilots. They thought I was weird."

"You were, dear. But in a good way." With that, Teresa gave Max another hug. "Let us know if you need anything at all. See you soon, Olivia."

"I've got to get to work," Olivia told Max. "With Kenneth on vacation, I'm in charge at the theater."

"Have you eaten lunch?" Max asked. When Olivia shook her head, Max said, "Like you said, you need to eat, right? How about I bring you lunch this time?"

"I'd love it. It'll give us a chance to talk more. I want

to spend as much time as possible with you before you leave."

"Aw, that's sweet." She hugged her friend goodbye and watched her walk out the front door. She was going to miss Olivia when she moved to New York.

Max took the teapot back to the office and put the cozy on it. They expected her to investigate the murder. What could it hurt to ask around and see what she could find out? She knew almost everyone in town, unlike Detective Cruz, which gave her a head start.

If she were a detective, where would she start? She couldn't wait for the toxicology reports, but she would be kind of working blind without them. She would question everyone the way Detective Cruz was, of course. She would start with Chad. Then perhaps Jennifer's mother, her coworkers and any friends she had. Her stomach grumbled, reminding her about lunch.

A quick call to her dad, and she had transportation arranged. In a small town like Crystal Shores, she could put up a sign that said, "Be back at..." with the little clock telling customers what time to expect her to return. She set it for 1:30. She walked the four blocks to her dad's house quickly, said hello, and grabbed the keys to his Mini Cooper. She'd already called ahead to the Bodhi Tree Café for veggie burgers, which she knew were Olivia's favorite.

Driving south down Coast Highway, Max passed the last Crystal Shores shop and had a clear view of the seashore for a mile or so. The sun glistened on the water, and several sailboats floated leisurely by. She turned right on Cliff Drive, and at the end of the street stood the Crystal Shores Playhouse. The theater, overlooking the ocean, had been built as a church in 1923. The congregation had grown so much by the Seventies that they moved into a huge new complex in Irvine. The old church sat abandoned and neglected for several years until a young Kenneth Chandler, now Darlene's husband, saw its potential as a theater. He raised the funds to renovate and convert it, and it had been a favorite of Orange County theatergoers ever since.

Max pulled into the parking lot, gathered up her bag of veggie burgers, and stepped out of the car. The theater stood proudly as if it had always been there, its cobblestone walls showing no wear. The wooden frames around the stunning cut glass windows appeared to need a fresh coat of paint. Kenneth depended on fundraisers and wealthy donors to pay for maintenance, and Max knew from Darlene that he struggled to keep a positive cash flow.

She walked up the stone steps and pulled open one of the enormous wooden doors, listening to it creak eerily. Entering the empty lobby, lit only by the sunlight filtering through the windows, she waited a moment for her eyes to adjust, and then entered the auditorium.

"Olivia?" she called out but heard only the echo of her footsteps as she walked down the center aisle and up the steps to the empty stage.

"Max! I thought I heard someone out here." Olivia came from behind a curtain.

"Hi Olivia." Max gave her friend a hug, and then noticed someone was behind her.

"Hello, Max," Chad said. He looked casually handsome in snug-fitting jeans and a white, long-sleeved t-shirt that made him look even more tan.

"How are you?" Max asked, and then wished she hadn't. What a stupid question to ask someone who just lost their fiancé.

"I'm doing okay, considering."

Max studied his face, looking for signs of grief. Were his eyes red from crying? She wasn't sure. Then she realized she was staring. "I hope I'm not interrupting anything."

"I was just leaving," Chad said, and Max watched him walk off the stage, down the aisle, and out the door.

Olivia took the bag from her and led her through a maze of hallways to her office. "You've never been backstage here, have you?"

"It's pretty cool." Max had never been in a play, but she loved theater, so the backstage area seemed magical to her. She followed Olivia into her office and looked around at all the posters that covered the walls showing old plays. "Where did you get all the posters?"

"I got some of them at antique stores, but most of them I found online. This is my favorite," she said, pointing out a poster of Laurence Olivier in Hamlet. "It's a reproduction, of course, but I still love it."

Clearing space on her desk and setting out the veggie burgers for them, Olivia handed Max a bottle of water and started to unwrap her burger.

"You're still shaken up about the murder, aren't you?" Olivia asked.

"What about you? You were friends with her." She took a long sip of water before asking what she really wanted to know. "By the way, what was Chad doing here?"

"He dropped off some of the files with the music for the play. He was helping us out, but of course, he has other things on his mind now, so I told him I'd find someone else to finish the editing."

"Did he say anything about losing Jennifer?"

"He didn't seem to want to talk about it, except to complain about her mother. She's not letting him be involved in the funeral arrangements," Olivia said. "You're awfully curious about him."

"I'm just trying to put all the pieces of the puzzle together." Max didn't want to tell her that Chad was one of her suspects. She knew Chad and Olivia were friends. "Do you know anyone who would want to harm her?" She had already unwrapped her burger and took a big bite.

"I knew it! You are investigating!"

Max gave her a sheepish look as she chewed her food. A few moments later, she could talk without her mouth full. "I figured it wouldn't hurt if I asked a few questions and see what I could find out. After all, I know pretty much everyone in town. You never know. I might learn something that would help the police in their investigation."

"I heard about the new detective. I hope he's more tolerant than the old one. He didn't appreciate you very much." Olivia took a bite of her burger. "Isn't this delicious?"

Max nodded tactfully. Veggie burgers weren't as good as the real thing, but this one didn't taste half bad. "The old detective had been on the force since I was a kid. He was just set in his ways. He didn't want me interfering."

"I'm glad he finally retired. What's the new one like?"

"Detective Cruz?" Max thought about how to reply. "He's okay, I think."

"What are you not telling me?" Olivia asked.

"Nothing." Except the part about how handsome he was. Time to change the subject. "Do you know if anyone had it out for Jennifer? You said everyone was pretty angry that she was shutting down the theater. Who was the most upset?"

"Probably Celeste."

Max grimaced at the name. When Max was fourteen, her mother accepted an invitation for her from Celeste's mother. It was a pool party. Celeste and her friends made fun of Max's one-piece bathing suit and skinny legs. They ganged up on her until she started to cry. Celeste's mother called her a baby and sent her home. The next day there was a pacifier tied to her locker. On the plus side, she was never invited to Celeste's house again

"She's our prima donna," Olivia continued. "She's been lobbying Kenneth to stage *Romeo and Juliet*. She's probably pushing so hard because she's getting too old for the part. Kenneth finally relented and it's on the schedule for this summer. It's Celeste's dream role."

"But there's no guarantee that whoever inherits the theater is going to renew the lease."

"No, but at the very least we'll be on a month to month until everything is sorted out. That will take a while, I'm sure."

Max thought Celeste didn't have a very strong motive, but it was still a motive. Celeste was so used to having her own way, who knows what she might do if someone stood in her way?

Max asked Olivia about *Arsenic and Old Lace*, their next production. Fiona and Teresa would be playing the murdering sisters. "Don't you think it's a little ironic that you're doing a play about women who go around poisoning people in light of what's happened?"

"I have thought about that. I'm not sure it's in good taste to go ahead with the show, but I don't think we have time to change it. We're already in rehearsals.

"It must be fun to work with Fiona and Teresa."

"Fiona's a kick. She played Lady Bracknell when we did *The Importance of Being Ernest*, and she had me in stitches half the time. I've never worked with Teresa, but she's such a sweetheart, I'm sure she'll be a joy. She totally nailed the audition."

"I can't wait to see it. I loved the movie."

"That's right. You and your old movies. Of course, you've seen it."

Looking around at all the old theater posters, Max said, "You're one to talk."

Olivia laughed. "Maybe that's why we get along so well. We're both stuck in the past."

"I'd love to live in the Twenties when they first built this place," Max admitted. "But only if I could bring my smartphone with me."

A loud knock interrupted their conversation, and the door flew open before Olivia could say, "Come in."

"I need to talk to you." It was Celeste, as beautiful as ever, with her mocha-colored skin and perfect thick, bouncy hair. "Oh, it's you," she said to Max.

"Can't it wait?" Olivia asked.

Celeste stood with her hands on her model-thin hips, which Max took to mean no.

"It's okay, Olivia. I need to get going." It was hard for Max not to say hello or acknowledge Celeste in some way, but her stubbornness won the battle over her polite nature. She hadn't spoken a word to Celeste in years and hoped to continue the tradition for years to come. As she walked down the hallway, she heard Celeste demanding that one of her costumes be changed.

Once she was back at the shop, Max knew she should get to work on the alterations she'd been procrastinating on while she was waiting for her next appointment, so she went to the workroom and started sewing.

Her two o'clock appointment arrived right on time. Susan Brown was a 35-year-old schoolteacher who lived in a duplex on Gardenia Street. She taught fourth grade at the local elementary school. Darlene had taken the call from Susan and seemed a bit miffed that Susan wanted to meet with Max. Apparently, there were many online reviews that mentioned her name, and she was starting to get calls from people who asked to see her and not Darlene.

She sat Susan down on the sofa and brought out a fresh pot of rose tea and two teacups.

"When did you get engaged, Susan?" Max asked, pouring tea into the cups.

"It's been one week as of today!" Her eyes sparkled.

"Well, tell me all about it." Max prompted. She held out a bowl of sugar cubes.

"If you insist!" Susan said, putting two sugar cubes into her cup. "I don't know if I'll ever get tired of recounting the story." She smiled contentedly as she stirred her tea. "Last September, I decided to get a personal trainer. You may think I'm not the type to work out, and you would be right, but I wanted to improve my cardiovascular fitness. It occurred to me if I had an appointment three times a week, I might have a better chance of achieving my goal. I would like to be able to go up a flight of stairs without getting winded. Or go for a hike in the hills."

"That's a smart idea." Max put a cube of sugar into her tea and thought maybe she should try that too. She had trouble keeping up with her dad when they went hiking, and he was thirty years older than she was.

"When I first met David West at the gym, I was dumbstruck. I mean I could hardly talk. He's not the most handsome man I've ever met, but there was something about him..."

"I know what you mean, believe me." For some reason, she thought of Detective Cruz.

"And remarkably, he says he felt the same when he met me." She beamed as she paused to take a sip of her tea. "Can you imagine a man who spends his days with all these women with perfect physiques falling for me?"

"I can totally imagine it! You are one of the nicest people I know," Max told her honestly. "And you're pretty too, of course."

"Thank you! David says it was my smile that made him fall for me. And I haven't stopped smiling since."

Max just nodded. She could tell Susan was in love. Someday she hoped to feel that way with someone who returned the feeling.

"It was our six-month anniversary…"

Susan told a rather typical story of a very nice dinner with champagne and a proposal over dessert. The way she told it, you could tell she thought it was the most special proposal ever. And it was, for her.

"Tell me your plans for the wedding," Max prompted.

They talked for fifteen minutes before they got on the subject of wedding dresses. Darlene always asked her why she took so long for her consultations, but she wanted to get a feel for her bride – were they romantic, no-nonsense, budget minded, or extravagant. It all helped her find or create the perfect dress.

Susan said she wanted to feel like a princess on her wedding day, and she'd brought a stack of pictures of poufy gowns with layers of tulle.

"When you say princess, are you thinking more Cinderella or Princess Grace?"

"Hmm. I hadn't thought about it that way." She looked a little embarrassed. "I suppose at my age I should want to look sophisticated or classy, or something, but I've dreamed of my wedding since I was a teenager. I want everything to be perfect. I suppose I simply want to feel like a princess."

"And we'll make sure you do." Max already had in her mind the perfect dress. She took the bride-to-be and the dress to the fitting room.

Susan was not a fru-fru kind of woman, so Max knew the right dress would make her feel like a princess without a lot of ruffles or embellishments. She went to the rack and considered several dresses similar to the ones in the pictures, but her gut told her they weren't right. She stood in front of the row of dresses and closed her eyes. She knew which one was right.

The dress she helped Susan into had a fitted, drop waist bodice and a sweetheart neckline. It was very slimming, and what woman doesn't appreciate that? There was just enough lace to keep it from being plain. The silk satin skirt flared out gently and swished softly as she walked.

She held Susan's hand as she stepped up on the platform. Susan was glowing just as she was when she told her about the proposal. She stared at herself in the mirror, and Max quietly waited.

Susan whispered, "It's perfect." She started to dab at her eye and Max handed her a box of tissues. Success.

Suddenly, Susan seemed to come out of a trance. "But how much? Can I afford it?"

"You most certainly can! It's within your budget, with enough left over for shoes and a headpiece."

Susan jumped off the platform and hugged Max.

"You better hand me some of those tissues," Max said.

They both started laughing as they dabbed at their moist eyes.

"How did you do it, Max? You're amazing! This gown isn't anything like the pictures I showed you, but it's absolutely perfect. I thought I was going to be trying on dresses all afternoon."

Max might not be a famous fashion designer yet, but this was pretty darn great. She helped dreams come true. How many people could say that? She was going to miss these moments.

CHAPTER 6

A young Asian woman in pigtails stuck her head in the door. "Oh, I am so sorry, you are busy," she said.

"Would you like to make an appointment?" Max asked.

"Oh, no. No need," the girl said and left the room.

While Max was helping Susan out of the dress, the phone rang. This was one of the reasons why they needed an assistant. The phone calls went to voice mail far too often, and then she had to stay late returning phone calls, usually catching people while they were eating dinner. While she took Susan's measurements to be sure to order the right size, she heard the phone ring again. When they went back into the front room, Max was surprised to see the young woman still in the shop.

Susan gave her another hug and left.

"May I help you?" Max asked.

"My name is Keiko. And you are Max Walters, is this correct?"

"Yes. It's nice to meet you, Keiko." She was wearing a gray plaid pleated skirt and a pink blazer over a white oxford shirt. Knee high socks and pink high tops completed the look.

"You have an appointment tomorrow at 10:30 with Tiffany Kerns," Keiko told her. "Your appointment book said you were available, but I told her you would call back to confirm."

"An appointment?" Max was confused.

"Yes, she called while you were busy. I assume answering the phone and making appointments are two of the duties of the job."

"Job?"

Keiko held out the sign that had been in the window. "You have an opening for an assistant. It says right here. I am interested in the position."

Max took the sign from Keiko. "Oh, yes. Well, it's only part time. Would you like to sit down?" She motioned to the overstuffed chairs. She hadn't expected to be interviewing anyone this week, with Darlene gone. The sign had been up for weeks, and no one had come in to apply for the job. Until now.

Keiko sat down primly, and Max sat across from her. "I am only available part time. Although I am on spring break this week, so I don't mind working more hours if needed. I can work ten a.m. to five p.m. this week. I understand you need extra help because the owner is on vacation? Next week, I can work one to five p.m. Is that all right with you?"

"I could use extra help this week." What questions should she ask? She'd never interviewed anyone before.

"But there is computer work as well. Are you familiar with computers?"

"I was a computer science major in college for two years."

"Just two years?" Max asked.

"I got bored."

"I see. Well, it can get a bit dull around here. There are a lot of menial tasks to do, like…" She noticed the teapot and cups were missing.

"The teapot is in your office," Keiko said. "I cleaned the cups. I put a funny knitted cap on the teapot. I think it will help keep the tea warm."

"Yes, well, thank you." Max thought for a moment. What would Darlene ask? "Actually, we were hoping to find someone who knew a little bit about fashion and fabrics."

"I attend the Orange County Fashion Design Institute. This is why I can only work part time. My last job was over the summer. My mother wanted me to focus on school and not work, but I told her I'm old enough to make my own decisions. I also have my own business designing websites." She reached into her bag. "Here is my resume and my references."

Max read the resume and reviewed the references. Everything seemed to be in order, although she couldn't help but think Keiko was overqualified for the job. She'd have to call the references, of course. Keiko was definitely different than their usual assistants. What would Darlene say? Keiko seemed to be perfect for the job, but maybe she should wait until Darlene got back. Still, she could definitely use the help this week. She decided to take the chance.

"Well, it will have to be on a trial basis because the owner is on vacation. She gave me her okay to hire someone, but I want her to meet you before we make it permanent." She smiled at the new assistant. "When can you start?"

"It seems I have already started." Keiko stood up as if she were ready to get to work.

"Yes, it does seem so. But I think there's some paperwork I need to do." Maybe Darlene had a file with whatever forms she needed.

"I can help you with that." Keiko reached into her messenger bag and pulled out a folder.

"That's an interesting bag. Is that a rabbit?" The bag was gray with two eyes, a mouth, and ears.

"That is *My Neighbor Totoro.*"

"Your neighbor?" Max asked.

"It's the name of a movie. Anime. From Japan. Hayao Miyazaki?"

Max stared at her blankly.

"Have you heard of the movie *Spirited Away? Howl's Moving Castle?* No? Well, never mind."

"Are you Japanese?" Max hoped she wasn't being rude by asking.

"Yes. My father lives in Japan. I live with my mother."

She handed Max a filled-out application, a W-2 form, and copies of her driver's license and social security card. "I think you will find these in order. Also, your father called and said he was having game night tonight and making lasagna. He invited me. May I come?"

"Sure, why not. You're not moving in or anything, are you?"

"Excuse me?"

"Never mind."

Just then the door jingled, and River came in.

"Hi, River."

"Hi, Max." River handed her a stack of mail.

"River, this is our new assistant, Keiko."

"Keiko, it's nice to meet you," River said. "I'm sure you will enjoy working with Max. She has talents of which she is not even aware."

"Yes, I believe she is very talented, which is why I wanted to work with her."

"I didn't know you had hired an assistant," River said to Max. "When did this happen?"

"About five minutes ago," Max answered.

"Well, when something's right, you just know it. Namaste," he said, and turned to go.

"Namaste?" Keiko looked puzzled.

"It's an ancient Sanskrit greeting. It means the spirit in me salutes the spirit in you," River explained.

"I see. I like it. Namaste," she said.

After River left, Max showed Keiko around the shop. The new assistant was full of questions. "I read online you are an excellent designer. Did you go to school or are you self-taught?"

"I learned a lot working for Darlene when I was a teenager. Then I went to design school in L.A. and still worked for Darlene in the summer. After I finished school, I moved to New York to work for Bissette as a pattern maker."

"I love their designs. Was it wonderful working for them?"

"Yes, and no." She opened the door to the office. "This is where we do all the ordering and emailing clients and suppliers. In fashion design, you really have to pay your dues and do a lot of menial jobs before you can actually do any designing."

"You got bored and quit?" Keiko asked. "I can understand that."

"Not exactly. It's true, the job wasn't exactly exciting, but my mother got sick. She had cancer. So, I moved back to help take care of her."

"I am so sorry. How is she?"

"She passed away almost six months ago. They didn't catch it in time." She blinked back the tears that always started when she talked about her mom. "And then my dad was all alone, and I was back working for Darlene, and I just kind of stayed." She closed the office door and walked down the hall and opened another door. "This is the workroom which is also the storeroom." She had created many beautiful gowns in this room. "These are the gowns that need altering," she said, pointing to three gowns hanging up in the back of the room.

"But now you are able to design. This is a much better job."

"Well, Darlene designs. I sew. And help run the shop. Let me show you the Dream Room."

"You design," Keiko said seriously. "Everyone knows it. If you wanted, you could open your own business."

"What? No, I don't need that kind of stress." She liked working for someone else and letting them handle all the big problems. Although, whenever there was a big problem, Darlene seemed to pass it on to her. Still, she didn't have to worry about paying the rent or the suppliers.

She was standing right where Jennifer had dropped dead. "I call this the Dream Room. This is where dreams come true."

"And sometimes end," Keiko added.

"What do you mean?"

"This is where Jennifer Burns collapsed last night, is it not?"

"You know about her?"

"Everyone knows. There was a headline in the paper, but not much in the way of details. I heard she was poisoned."

"That's what it looks like," Max said, wondering how Keiko had already heard the rumor about Jennifer being poisoned.

"Was it scary?"

"Not at the time." Max remembered how she felt when Jennifer was lying on the floor. "Well, I did panic a bit. I just thought she passed out because the bodice was too tight. Plus, the woman probably never eats. I mean, ate. Oh man, I'm such a bad person, talking like that about someone who's dead."

"From what I have heard, she was not a very nice person."

"No, well, but I'm sure she had redeeming qualities. I just have no idea what they were." They walked back into the showroom. "How's your sewing?" she asked Keiko.

"I can sew well," Keiko answered. "I want to be better at taking an idea in my head and turning it into a garment. That is why I wanted to work with you. From what I have heard, you can create anything."

"I don't know about that." She wondered how this young girl seemed to know so much about her. She'd have to go online and see what was written about her.

"I think perhaps you do not even know what you can do. Me, on the other hand, I know I have wonderful ideas. But when I create them, they are not so wonderful."

"I'd love to see some of your sketches," Max said politely.

"Great!" Keiko lit up. "I have them right here." She stopped. "I mean is now okay?"

"Sure, why not?" She smiled at Keiko's enthusiasm.

Keiko pulled a sketchbook out of her bag. The first page was an exquisite drawing of a sleek, off the shoulder gown with long flowing sleeves. It was painted in earth-tone watercolors, and in the background, you could see a castle in the distance. Max just stared at it.

"There are more," Keiko said.

Max turned the pages, looking at the most imaginative designs she had seen in a long time. The pictures looked like illustrations for a fantasy novel.

"They're really wonderful," Max said softly. "I wish I could draw as well as you."

"I can help you!" Keiko paused, and shyly added, "I mean if you wanted me to."

"I'd love it." She paged through the sketchbook, admiring the beautiful drawings. She stared at one of the pictures. "Your designs are so artistic. I wonder if you wouldn't be better suited to costume design."

Keiko sighed and pouted. "I want real people to wear my designs. Real people who want to feel extraordinary and want their clothes to reflect that."

"Well, I can help you make them more wearable," Max told her. "I mean, if you wanted me to."

"I would be most happy to get your advice." Keiko looked around. "Now, what else do you have to show me?"

Max wondered what she should show Keiko next. Then she remembered something. "Have you ever seen handmade lace from Ireland?"

She took Keiko into the workroom and opened the package from Ireland. She unfolded the lace, and the two of them admired it.

"It's like spider webs," Keiko said.

"I know. Isn't it interesting? I don't even know what I'm going to use it for, but I had to have it."

Max showed Keiko her lace collection, which she kept in an antique dresser in the workroom. Darlene scolded her for spending money on lace that wasn't for a particular dress, but she found it much easier to show their bride's actual lace swatches rather than pictures. Usually, she ordered just a swatch or an eighth of a yard, but the Irish lace was only available as a yard or more. And it wasn't cheap. She'd be in for a lecture for sure.

The next few hours flew by with no further interruptions except for a number of phone calls from people curious to hear more about the murder.

They went back into the office, and Max showed Keiko the client management system. She had Keiko enter Tiffany Kerns' information. Keiko then showed Max how the system had the ability to set appointments. She set one up for Tiffany.

Max was enjoying working with Keiko. She was bright and curious, with lots of questions about the business and designing. Max almost felt bad about leaving to go to New York. She wondered if she should tell Keiko, but she decided she should tell Darlene first. At least, that was her excuse. She just didn't want to tell Keiko right now while things were going so well.

Keiko stopped in the middle of a question and said, "Your phone is not charging." She fiddled with the connections. "There, now it is."

"No wonder no one has called me on my cell. Of course, everyone who really knows me knows half the time I've either forgotten to charge my phone or left it at home."

"Do you ever forget important things, like ordering a dress?" Keiko wondered.

"No, never! I am utterly focused on my brides. And I make notes and reminders in the computer. Notice all the sticky notes?" She pointed to the yellow notes stuck around the monitor. "Darlene hates them, but she has learned to live with them."

Keiko picked up a vase from the desk. "What are all these colored stones?" The vase was half full of frosted pieces of glass.

"Those are sea glass. For decades, trash has ended up in the sea. The ocean takes a broken piece of glass, turns it into this and deposits it back on the shore. Isn't nature remarkable?" Max took a green, irregularly shaped piece about an inch long out of the vase and showed it to Keiko. "The sand and the currents smooth off all the sharp edges and gives it a frosted appearance. I think they're beautiful. Most of them are white, green and amber. It's rarer to find a blue or red piece."

"Did you find all this glass yourself?" Keiko asked.

"Most of it. Plus, everyone knows I collect it, so they bring me pieces. Sometimes after a storm, I'll come back with a handful. That reminds me." She pulled the red gemstone out of her pocket. "I found this yesterday morning on the beach while I was hunting for sea glass."

Keiko took the stone from Max and turned it over in her palm. She stared at it for a while as if spellbound. "Maybe it's a Chintamani," she whispered.

"A what?"

"A Chintamani. A wishing stone." She squinted at Max. "Have you made any wishes since you found it?"

"I did wish I had an assistant."

"And you got one! It is a Chintamani!"

"Hold on," Max said. She took the stone from Keiko.

"I wish a handsome, eligible man would walk through the door." The jingling of the door startled them.

"Hi, Max," Eric called out from the showroom.

"See," Keiko said loudly. "It is a Chintamani!"

"What's up?" Eric asked, sticking his head in the office. "What's a Chintawhoosit?"

"Eric, this is Keiko. Keiko, meet Eric. He owns Flower to the People. It's just a block down the street. He's also my very good friend."

"Am I interrupting a consultation?" he asked. "I can come back later."

"Keiko's my new assistant. I just hired her."

"Awesome! Welcome, Keiko." He turned to Max. "You hired her without Darlene's approval? Good for you! How long do you think...?" He stopped mid-sentence.

"Apparently, I wished for her. So, I get to keep her as long as I want." She wasn't ready to tell Eric she was moving back to New York. She wanted to wait until they had some time alone.

"You wished for her?" Eric raised his eyebrows.

"She found a Chintamani," Keiko explained. "A wishing stone."

"A wishing stone. Uh-huh." Eric did not appear at all convinced.

"Some say it fell from the sky, or that it comes from the dragon king of the sea," Keiko said. "That's why you found it on the beach." She said it like it was the obvious conclusion.

"Oh my god!" Max cried out suddenly. "I wished her dead. Right before she collapsed."

"What did you say?" Keiko asked. "Do you remember?"

"I said 'I wish you'd drop dead,' or something like that. I killed her!"

"Hush!" Eric said. "Be careful saying things like that. Someone's bound to hear you and take you seriously. Let me see it." He took the stone from her.

"It's just a garnet. I'm sure of it. But if you want to call it a Chinta..."

"Chintamani," Keiko said.

"If you want to call it a Chintamani, then go for it."

"Wait a second." Max grabbed Eric's arm. "I should wish for world peace."

"You only get three wishes," Keiko said. "How many did you make?"

"Only three wishes? But I've already made three wishes! I wasted them."

"I don't know," Keiko said. "You got me."

"True," Max agreed. "Besides, when you think about it, if world peace could happen by someone wishing for it, it would have happened by now."

"Well, this has been fascinating, but I'd better get back to the shop." Eric gave Max another hug. "I left Daphne in charge and that's never a good idea. She can't tell a pansy from a petunia."

"So, why do you keep her?"

"She's entertaining," he said and went out the door.

"I wonder why he stopped by," Max wondered out loud.

"You wished for him," Keiko replied. "Now where were we?"

The rest of the afternoon flew by, and at six o'clock, Max turned the sign around to the closed side. When she started up the vacuum, Keiko took it from her and ran it once around the shop. After she finished and put the vacuum away, Max opened the front door to leave when Keiko said, "Are you forgetting something?"

Max was confused.

"Your phone?"

She went back to the office and grabbed it off the charger.

CHAPTER 7

When Max and Keiko entered her father's front door, they were greeted with the delicious smell of lasagna, fresh out of the oven. She introduced Keiko and accepted a glass of white wine from her dad. He tried to give one to Keiko, who seemed about to accept it when Max told him she was only twenty. They sat down at the oversized dining table, and Max noticed there were eight plates in a stack.

"Who else is coming?" Game night was an open invitation to all their friends and neighbors, so there was no telling who was going to show up.

"Fiona and Teresa are coming. Eric said he'd try to stop by. Olivia said she was too busy at the theater with Kenneth gone, so she can't come. I left Andy a message for him and Stacy to stop by, but I didn't hear back, so I don't know if they'll make it."

There was a knock on the door and the McNulty

sisters entered. Max introduced Keiko to the two women.

"How are things at the yarn shop?" Richard asked.

"Slow. You know, we're not in it for the money," Fiona told him, and Teresa nodded. "We just like somewhere to go every day and we like to keep busy."

"And we love knitting," Teresa added. "It's so relaxing."

"But it doesn't make sense to keep it open if it continues to lose money," Fiona continued. "We're thinking of closing up the shop. I just feel bad for our customers. We're one of the few shops that carry some of the more expensive yarns, like cashmere and angora."

"Plus, you have those wonderful organic, hand-dyed yarns," Max said. "They're very popular. The colors are so beautiful, it makes me wish I could knit." Max hoped they wouldn't close the shop. She loved having them next door.

"Yes, Fiona dyes them herself," Teresa explained. "There are very few places you can find anything like them. People with allergies and skin sensitivities tell us they're a godsend."

"You need a website," Keiko piped in. "You'd get plenty of business if you had one."

"We've thought of it," Fiona admitted. "We just don't know how to go about it. Plus, isn't it expensive?"

"I will see you at 5:15 tomorrow," Keiko told them, "And I will have a website for you in a week. You will only pay me if you make money from it."

The sisters glanced at each other, then back at Keiko.

"You are free at 5:15?" Keiko asked.

"Oh, yes. We're free," Fiona said. She pulled Max aside and asked, "Where did you find her?"

"She found me," Max said. "After I wished for her."

Before the sisters could ask what she meant, Eric arrived with a bouquet of peonies that he handed to Richard. Richard put them in a vase, which he placed in the center of the table.

Everyone grabbed a seat, and Max poured wine for everyone but Keiko, who had some of Richard's honey-sweetened iced green tea. Max helped her dad put the lasagna and salad on the counter and everyone helped themselves.

"The lasagna is delicious, Richard," Fiona said, and Teresa, Eric, and Keiko murmured in agreement, unable to talk since their mouths were full. "I'd ask you for the recipe, but I haven't done much cooking since my husband passed away."

"I'm sorry," Keiko said.

"Oh, thank you dear, but it's been almost ten years now. I had thirty good years with him. I have two wonderful sons and three grandchildren. And, of course, I have Teresa."

"I'll send you home with some leftovers," Richard offered.

"It's even better the next day," Max said. "So, make sure you save some for me, Dad!"

As they passed around the garlic bread, they talked about flowers and antiques and the painting Richard was working on, an oil painting of a little girl and her mother on the beach.

"I saw one of your paintings in the window of the gallery," Eric said. "It's beautiful."

"It will probably be there until summer. The tourists love the seascapes, but this time of year I don't sell a lot."

"Lots of people in Crystal Shores have your paintings on their walls," Eric told him.

"I do," Max said, grabbing another piece of buttery garlic bread.

"Yes, but you didn't pay for it," Richard said, laughing.

"But I would." She paused. "Well, if I could afford it, that is. It's lovely. And it matches my sofa perfectly. Of course, that's because I made the slipcovers to match the painting."

They ate in silence until Fiona spoke. "Well, if no one else is going to bring it up, I will. Any news on Jennifer's murder?" she asked Max.

"You mean her suspicious death?" Max relayed all she knew, which wasn't much.

Teresa asked, "Do you think the murderer is someone who lives in Crystal Shores?"

"The police haven't ruled it a homicide," Max said, "but if it was murder, it seems likely that it's someone in town. If we could trace Jennifer's steps before she got to the shop, maybe we could figure out who was near enough to poison her."

"Spoken like a true detective," Fiona said.

MURDER IN WHITE LACE

"Oh--I was just being theoretical. I'm guessing that's what the police are doing now."

"I wouldn't be surprised if you figured it out before the police," Eric joined in.

Richard crossed his arms and said sternly, "Max will let the police handle this. This isn't another missing person or lost watch. This is dangerous."

"Of course, Richard," Eric said. "I only meant..."

"I know. Max has something of a sixth sense when it comes to figuring out the truth, which is why I never could lie to her. She was five when she accused me of lying about Santa Claus."

Eric added, "I once told her I loved her outfit, just to be nice, and she saw right through me." Everyone laughed.

Once they'd finished eating and the dishes were cleared, Richard started to set up the game on the table. Keiko walked over to the fireplace mantel.

"Is this a picture of your mom?" she asked. When Max said it was, Keiko said, "She was beautiful."

Max glanced at her dad, who smiled at her wistfully. "Yes, she was," she said.

"And smart," Richard said, "and loving, and thoughtful..." His voice trailed off.

"And a wonderful friend," Fiona said, while Richard excused himself and left the room. Max knew he wanted to compose himself. She blinked back tears of her own.

"I'm sorry," Keiko said. "I didn't mean to upset him."

"Don't ever be sorry about reminding us about my mom. He just needs a moment."

Everyone took seats around the table and Max finished setting up the game.

"Well, Max, since Richard's out of the room," Fiona said, "we can talk about who we think murdered Jennifer. Do you think it was someone we know?"

"It's almost certainly someone Jennifer knew, so it's a good chance we know them too."

"Did all of you know Jennifer?" Keiko asked, then quickly added, "I'm not saying any of you killed her!"

Eric told Keiko. "I went to school with Jennifer. Middle school and high school. She was always trying to be in with the popular girls, but she didn't have that much money, unlike a lot of the kids in town. And you know how some kids turn up their noses at the ones who don't have nice stuff. She got a job in high school, and I think she spent all her money on clothes. She was always trying to keep up with everyone."

"Didn't she move to New York to be a model?" Fiona asked.

"Yeah, right after she divorced her first husband. That marriage only lasted about six months," Eric answered. "When she was in New York, I think she spent more time partying than modeling. Then she came back a few years later and married William Chase."

"His family owns half of Crystal Shores," Max explained to Keiko.

"William had plenty of money and property of his own," Eric added. "They got him started in his own real estate firm. They met when Jennifer went to work for him."

"Does he still own the firm?" Max asked.

"He sold it after he divorced Jennifer."

"Did Jennifer still work there when she..." Keiko didn't seem to know how to finish the sentence. Max knew how hard it was to say the words 'she died'.

"Yes," Eric answered. "And she was very successful, from what I've heard."

"We didn't really know Jennifer, but we know her mother," Fiona said, and Teresa nodded. "Sonia goes to Tai Chi class with us at the senior center. I called and left her a message today and told her we'd stop by to pay our respects tomorrow. How sad to lose your daughter. She must be heartbroken and in shock. I don't think Sonia had any other children, and her husband passed away a few years ago. She must be devastated."

Richard came back to the table and passed out cups of coffee and set out cream and sugar.

Max took a cookie and sipped her coffee, deep in thought. She hoped her dad had made decaf or she'd be up all night thinking about who might have killed Jennifer. A pounding on the door interrupted her reverie. She rushed to the door and let Stacy in. She was in tears.

"The police arrested Andy!"

CHAPTER 8

*S*tacy sat on the sofa, dabbing her tear-streaked face with a tissue. She took a big gulp of the cognac Richard offered her and started coughing. Max ran over to pat her on the back, and Richard hurried into the kitchen for a glass of water.

Everyone hovered around her, waiting expectantly.

"What the heck is that?"

"It's cognac," Richard said, holding out a glass of water. "I take it you don't drink much."

"That's strong stuff!" She stared at the glass as if it were something dangerous, and then took a tiny sip. She grimaced and handed it back to Richard in exchange for the water.

"What happened?" Richard asked.

"The police showed up at the bakery just after we closed with a warrant for Andy's arrest. His parents had to stand there and watch him being handcuffed and taken away. It was horrible!"

"Stacy, why have they arrested Andy?" Richard asked.

"I reckon they think he killed Jennifer." She started to sob quietly, then shook her head and took a deep breath. "No. I gotta be strong. For Andy."

"Where did they take him?" Max was outraged that anyone could think Andy could hurt anyone. She was going to give that Detective Cruz a piece of her mind. Imagine! Andy in jail!

"They took him to the police station. They wouldn't let me see him, so I came on over here." Everyone was gathered around her. "I was hopin' to see you Max, but you weren't at your place. What are y'all doin' here?"

"It's game night," Max said. "Dad said he invited you."

"Oh, dangit. I forgot."

"Not surprising." Max put her arm around Stacy. "What can we do to help?"

"Andy's folks are at the police station waitin' for the lawyer. I oughta go back soon. I don't know when they're gonna let me see him."

"If there's anything we can do," Richard said, "you just let us know."

"They'll need to press charges, or they can't hold him for long," Max said.

"What if they charge him for murder?" Stacy said. "Then what am I going to do?"

"In that case, his lawyer will get him out on bail," Max said. "And they'll soon figure out he had nothing to do with Jennifer's death."

Stacy grabbed both of Max's arms. "But what if they

don't. Here's what I was thinking. You're real good at findin' things. Find the real murderer."

Max was silent, not sure what to say.

Richard frowned. "Stacy, that's a job for the police."

Max saw the hope drain from Stacy's face. Her eyes looked down and she turned her head away.

"What am I gonna do? What if he goes to jail for good?" Stacy began to sob again.

"I'm sure they'll let him go soon," Max tried to reassure her. "They can't have any evidence against him." But she knew they wouldn't have arrested him without evidence. There were the cake samples. Had they tested them already? There couldn't possibly be poison in them, but why else would the police have arrested Andy? "Did the police mention any evidence?"

Stacy grabbed Max's arm. "They didn't say anything, but they musta had evidence. They wouldn't have arrested him if they didn't, right? What if they give him the death penalty?" She was becoming more agitated as she spoke.

Richard asked, "Why do the police think Andy's guilty?"

"That's just it. I don't know a thing. I haven't got to talk to Andy yet, and the police wouldn't tell us anything."

Stacy's tear-streaked face almost broke Max's heart. "I'll see if I can get any more information from the police." It wasn't much, but Max couldn't watch Stacy suffer without doing something.

"You will? Bless you!" Stacy hugged her tightly,

making it hard to breathe. "I need to get back to the police station and find out if I can see Andy."

"I'll walk you out," Max said. She and Stacy stood up, and each of their friends gave Stacy a hug goodbye and wished her good luck.

Once Max had Stacy alone in the front patio, she quizzed her.

"Okay, tell me everything you know. What did the police say when they arrested Andy?"

Stacy thought. "They said, 'You're under arrest. You have the right to remain silent.'"

"Um, what did they say about why they arrested him?"

"They said they were arresting him for murder."

"Did they say why?"

"No, but I think it's 'cause they think he killed Jennifer."

Max shook her head. "Yes, I figured as much. Did they say why they thought he was guilty?"

"I don't remember. I don't think so. That's all I know." She twisted the handle of her purse, anxious to go.

Max gave her a long hug. "Let me know if you find out anything else, okay?"

"Okay," Stacy said and hurried to her car.

Once she was back inside, everyone sat down again at the dining room table, but no one made a move to start the game. Max thought about Andy at the police station. Was he sitting in a hard metal chair in an inter-rogation room like on TV? Was Cruz questioning him now, recording every word, waiting for Andy to say something incriminating? She hoped he didn't say anything until the lawyer arrived.

"What an awful day," Richard said. "Or I should say two days. Andy's in jail, and that poor woman is dead."

Max heard a phone ringing and realized it was coming from her purse hanging off the back of her chair. The ringtone was different, which was weird. But her phone seemed to have a mind of its own, so it didn't surprise her. She took it out and answered, "Hello."

"Who is this?" a man's voice asked.

"You called me." Max couldn't place the voice, although it sounded familiar. "Who are you?"

"This is Detective Cruz. Is this Max?"

"Yes." Why was he calling her? "Who did you expect?"

"What are you doing with Jennifer's phone?" he asked, sounding irritated.

"I don't have Jennifer's phone." She tried to think. What had she done with Jennifer's phone the night she died? "At least I'm pretty sure I don't have it."

"You're talking on it."

Max held the phone away from her face and stared at it for a moment. It looked just like her phone. It was the latest iPhone. She'd just upgraded from her four-year-old phone when it finally died. She'd been meaning to get a case for it but couldn't decide which one to get.

She got back on the phone. "Then where's my phone?" she asked.

"I have it. We picked it up from the shop, thinking it

was Jennifer's phone. Once we charged it, we realized it was yours. Where are you?" he demanded.

Max gave him her dad's address and hung up.

"Boy, he was testy," she said

"What was that about?" Richard asked.

"Turns out this is Jennifer's phone. He's coming over to pick it up. It's just like mine. I hope he's bringing mine." There could be texts or emails on the phone that would point to the murderer. Max pressed the menu button and the phone asked for a password. She stared at it, wondering what password Jennifer might have used. Her wedding date? Max put in the five digits, but the phone buzzed at her, and the screen said, 'try again.'

"Isn't that the latest iPhone?" Eric asked. "I can't believe you have the latest technology. Remember that flip phone you had forever?"

"I hated giving it up, but it died on me," Max admitted. "It was so simple and easy to use. But the new one is great." She actually resented having to spend time learning to use it. She missed the days when a phone was just a phone.

Fiona leaned over and whispered in Max's ear just as Keiko took the phone from her and walked into the kitchen. "Do you think Detective Cruz will tell you anything about the investigation?" Fiona asked.

Max shrugged, looking over her shoulder to see what Keiko was up to. What would she be doing with Jennifer's phone? Was she trying to find evidence? Or was she up to something else? Max turned back to Fiona. "I don't think he likes me."

"Nonsense." Fiona pulled out a chair and sat next to her. "Everyone likes you."

They talked about Andy and how ridiculous it was that he was suspected of murder. Everyone but Keiko had known him since he was a kid. Everyone at the table had at least one story to tell about what a great guy Andy was. He had never been in the slightest bit of trouble. He had a paper route in his pre-teens and then mowed lawns for extra money. One of the senior citizens in town couldn't afford to pay him so he did it for free. She gave him cookies and milk to thank him. Max remembered he said the cookies were almost inedible, but he ate them anyway because he didn't want to hurt her feelings.

"I feel so helpless," Fiona said. "I wish there were something I could do to help Andy. He's such a nice young man. I just hate the thought of him in prison."

Max didn't even want to think about Andy in prison, but she couldn't help thinking they must have some kind of evidence against him to arrest him. What could it possibly be? And how could she find out?

She looked around for Keiko. What was she doing with the phone? What if she did something with it and Max got blamed for it? She went into the kitchen, but Keiko wasn't there.

"Max? Keiko?" Max heard her dad calling from the dining room. "Let's get started before it gets too late."

"I don't know where Keiko went."

"Maybe she just stepped out for some fresh air," Richard said.

Even though no one seemed that interested in

playing a game, Max sat back down at the dining room table and picked out a game piece. Richard read the rules for the game, which started to get Max's mind off Andy's troubles. Keiko sat down next to her and handed her the phone. She started to ask what she was doing with it when the doorbell rang. Detective Cruz entered. Max could feel the hostility in the room toward the detective who had arrested their friend and neighbor. Cruz nodded as he surveyed the room.

"Are you having a meeting?" the detective asked.

"It's game night. We get together the first Tuesday of every month. My wife started the tradition. There's more lasagna, Detective, if you're hungry," Richard said. Max wondered why he was being so nice.

"Thanks, Richard," the detective said. "That's very kind of you. I just stopped by to get Jennifer's phone."

Max got up from the table. "It's right here. Here you go." She handed the phone to Cruz.

"What are you up to, Max?" Cruz asked.

"Up to? Why would I be up to anything?" Max didn't even try to hide her anger. "I'm just having a nice evening with friends. By the way, Andy is not guilty."

"If you have any evidence of that, then, by all means, share it with me. If not, the best way to help your friend is by not interfering with the investigation." The detective shook his head slowly. "That goes for all of you," he announced.

Everyone nodded silently. After the detective left, Fiona and Teresa got up to go. But before they reached the front door, Fiona said, "I bet you figure out who the murderer is before he does."

"You heard what he said. He basically told me to stay out of it."

"But you won't stop thinking about it," Teresa said. "I know you."

Max said goodnight to the two women, then came back to the table. "Well, I guess game night was a bust."

Richard said, "That's okay. It's just an excuse to get together. And I'm glad I got to meet you, Keiko."

Keiko grinned. "Can I come again next time?"

"You have an open invitation," Richard assured her, putting the game back in the box.

"What were you doing with her phone?" Max asked Keiko.

"I was just curious about what information she might have on it. Like her schedule. Now I know what she had planned on the day she died."

"Why did you want to know her schedule?" Richard asked.

"Has it not occurred to anyone here that if Andy is cleared, and none of you seem to think he is capable of murder, that Max could be a suspect?"

"A suspect?" Max was shocked. "What motive could I possibly have?"

"Everyone has secrets," Keiko said.

"I don't have any secrets," Max said.

Keiko stared at her, and Max stared back. "Okay, it's not like I tell everyone everything, but I certainly didn't have any motive to kill Jennifer."

Richard said, "I'm sure there's no way you could be a suspect."

Max hoped he was right. "Anything telling in her schedule?" she asked Keiko.

"Not much. Mostly some appointments with clients. She had lunch at Chez Mer and an appointment at Salon Fred."

"That's Salon Frederique. It's a nail salon."

"She also had an appointment with a florist, then a date at a place called the Cheshire Cat. Is that a restaurant?"

"It's a gastropub. It's the latest thing." Max saw Keiko's blank look and added, "It's a bar and restaurant." She turned to Eric. "Were you the florist she was meeting?"

"Yes. Her appointment was for 5:00, but of course, she was late."

"No surprise there." Max remembered he had told Detective Cruz that he hadn't seen her since last week. What was he hiding?

"Well, I'd better run," Eric said abruptly, which made Max more suspicious. He pulled Max aside. "Can I get a rain check on dinner tomorrow?"

What was going on with Eric? First lying to the police and then ditching her for dinner. "We need to talk."

"I can explain," he said. "I'll talk to you tomorrow."

"So why are you canceling our dinner?"

"I have a date!"

"That's great." Eric hadn't dated since his last serious relationship ended nearly a year ago. "It's about time you started dating again. But we still need to talk."

"We will." He hugged her. "I promise."

After everyone had left, Max was left alone with her dad. She curled up on the sofa, and he sat in his favorite chair.

"I don't want you getting involved," Richard said.

"Who said I was getting involved?" It wasn't a lie, but she had to admit to herself she wanted to find out who murdered Jennifer. She wanted to help Andy if she could, but also her curiosity was getting the better of her.

"I promised your mom I would keep you safe. She was the one who made sure nothing bad ever happened to us while I was busy being a free spirit. She worried about you, you know."

Max's eyes glistened and she smiled. "I always told her she had nothing to worry about, but that didn't stop her."

"She worried so much when you moved to New York. Afraid you were going to get mugged or get taken advantage of. Of course, she worried you were going to get your heart broken ever since you were a teenager. I always told her you were levelheaded, and not a bit like me."

They sat quietly, each in their own thoughts.

"Who do you think killed Jennifer?" she asked, and when he just frowned at her she added, "I'm just wondering, that's all."

Richard shook his head. "I have no idea. You?"

"Me neither. Her fiancé Chad seems the most likely suspect. I'm pretty sure he was marrying her for her money, but then wouldn't he wait until he married her to bump her off?"

"You're just being theoretical, right?" he said, with worry in his voice.

"Just thinking out loud," she said, purposely not making any promises. Someone had to clear Andy's name. "I'm sure Andy's parents have gotten him the best lawyer in town. If they charge Andy with murder, the police will stop looking at anyone else." If the detective wasn't looking into other suspects, someone needed to. She felt her dad's eyes on her. "Oh, don't look at me like that. You can't expect me to stop thinking about it."

She kissed her dad on the cheek and went out the back door and up the stairs to her apartment. She felt emotionally exhausted but wide awake. She put on her pajamas and crawled into bed with a notebook. She made a list of everyone who knew Jennifer, at least everyone she was aware of. She was too tired to come up with any theories, but she was too worried about Andy to sleep.

She got up out of bed, microwaved a mug of warm milk, and turned on the TV. She checked out the movies on demand and found *My Neighbor Totoro*. She was halfway through it when she fell asleep on the sofa. She woke up in the middle of the night and crawled into bed.

CHAPTER 9

$\mathcal{M}$ ax opened one eye and peered at the clock. 6:15. She groaned, rolled over, and tried to go back to sleep. She felt as if she had awoken from a bad dream. She rolled over again and then sat up in bed, eyes wide open. Andy had been arrested for murder!

She felt powerless and yet she knew she had to do something. Crawling out of bed, she threw on a pair of black yoga pants, a purple t-shirt, and sneakers. She got the coffee out of the cupboard and then realized she didn't have any filters. Within minutes she stepped through her dad's back door. She smelled the coffee as soon as she entered the kitchen.

"What are you doing up so early?" she asked.

"I don't always sleep in 'till nine. I have yoga class this morning. I'm making pancakes. Want some?"

"Sure, that'd be great." She wasn't sure she'd eat pancakes before going to yoga, but she chose to keep her mouth shut, at least until the pancakes were on her plate.

"Did you sleep okay?" he asked, with concern in his voice.

"Do I look that bad? Don't answer. I couldn't get to sleep last night. I'm worried about Andy. I wish I could do something."

"Let the police do their job, Max. They'll find the real killer."

She knew her dad was probably right, but she couldn't stop worrying that Andy could spend a long time in jail for a murder he didn't commit. She shuddered.

"I keep thinking about all the people who hated her," she wondered out loud. "One of them must have hated her enough to want her dead."

"Okay, I can't stop you from thinking about it, but if you come up with any real suspicions, let the police know. I'm worried enough about Andy. I don't need to be worrying about you too."

"Sure, Dad. I won't do anything stupid. I promise."

After some delicious, fluffy pancakes with pure maple syrup, Max helped her dad do the dishes. "Is it too early to call Andy's parents and ask what's going on?"

"I already called them. I figured they wouldn't be sleeping in late. They're still holding Andy, but they only have 24 hours to charge him or let him go."

"I'll stop in at the bakery later," Max said. "Hope-fully, they've released him by then. I'm going to walk down to the beach." She finished the last of her coffee and put the cup in the dishwasher. "The sound of the waves always helps me clear my head."

She went back to her place to get a sweatshirt. She grabbed her notebook and pen and walked the two blocks to the beach. The fog was taking a break this morning, and the bright sun glistened on the water. Passing a young couple enjoying the view from a park bench, she walked down the staircase that led down the cliff to the sand. She took off her sneakers and her feet sank into the cool sand. When she got close to the water, she plunked down on the sand and opened her notebook.

Andy Fuller was her first entry, and next to it she wrote: *police #1 suspect. Grew up in Crystal Shores. Met wife Stacy at Humboldt State University. Decided not to become a doctor but take over family bakery. Went on one date with Jennifer a few years ago, before he married Stacy.*

Next: Stacy Fuller. *Grew up in Corpus Christi, Texas.* She didn't know much more about Stacy.

She had Jennifer's fiancé Chad Stevenson's name on the list, as well as William Chase, her ex-husband. Their divorce was ugly, she'd heard. She wondered where he was living now, so she wrote the question next to his name.

Eric couldn't stand Jennifer, and they certainly had history. Eric had confided that Jennifer had spread rumors about him being gay at Crystal Shores High School where they both attended six years before Max attended the same school. It broke Max's heart hearing about how he was bullied. She stared at his name on her list. Even if he were capable of murder, why would he kill her now? They were getting along enough for Eric to do the flowers for her wedding. But he had lied about seeing her the day she died. She didn't for a moment think that Eric had anything to do with the murder, but she did need to find out the truth. She wrote a few notes next to his name.

Keiko wasn't on her list. It made no sense that a murderer would apply for a job in the same shop where their victim had succumbed. Plus, she had no indication that the two women had ever met. Although it was an odd coincidence that she showed up the day after the murder. Keiko almost seemed too good to be true. Was she? Was Max blinded by her youth and apparent innocence? Max shook her head. She was starting to suspect everyone.

Next on her list were Fiona and Teresa, two sweet little old ladies who owned a knitting shop and did occasional community theater. They were going to be in Arsenic and Old Lace soon. They both knew Jennifer's mother but barely knew Jennifer at all, as far as she was aware.

Max stared at the page. She wouldn't get anywhere if she didn't keep an open mind. Plus, the police would be checking out everyone after they let Andy go, which she told herself they would have to do soon, so she needed to do the same. She added Keiko to the list, and then she wrote her own name. As Keiko had pointed out, the police could consider her a suspect once they realized Andy didn't kill Jennifer. But Max had no motive.

But who did have a motive? Not just for killing

Jennifer, but for killing Jennifer *now*. Did it have something to do with the upcoming wedding? Who would benefit from her death? She needed to find out who was going to inherit her estate. Was it her mother, Chad, or someone else entirely?

Max closed her notebook and headed back home. She still had plenty of time before she had to get ready for work, so she got out the stew meat and vegetables she had bought on Sunday. She could throw everything in the crock-pot and have dinner ready when she got home.

After her shower, she put on a pair of black slacks, white tank top, and a peach-colored cardigan sweater and she was ready to go.

When she got to the bridal shop she kept going and headed for the bakery two doors down. When she stepped inside, Stacy was helping a line of customers, and Andy's parents were nowhere to be seen. She got in line so she could talk to Stacy. Plus, their coffee was really good, and after getting so little sleep last night, she figured another cup wouldn't hurt.

"Hi Max," Stacy said when she got to the front of the line. Her eyes looked red like she'd been crying all night. "You look like you could use a cup of coffee."

"Yes, I didn't sleep well," Max admitted. "A large dark roast, please." When Stacy came back with the coffee, Max handed her a five and whispered so no one else would hear, "Did they release him?"

Stacy just shook her head sadly and handed Max her change.

"I'll check back with you later," Max said, wishing she could give Stacy a hug.

She walked back to her shop, wondering how Andy was holding up. She couldn't imagine what he was going through.

In spite of everything, she still had a shop to run. Every morning when she got to work, Max went over her schedule for the day. Tiffany, the new client who had called yesterday was on the schedule. Max had never met her, so she had no idea what to expect, but she was excited to meet with Tiffany without Darlene looking over her shoulder. Susan had an appointment at one o'clock with her Maid of Honor to pick out bridesmaid dresses. Susan was on spring break and trying to get as much done as possible this week. Max had asked her to bring in full-length pictures of all the women in her bridal party.

She headed for the front door to unlock it when Keiko knocked. She was wearing a pink flowered dress with a fur capelet, white tights, and high-heeled Mary Janes. Her hair was down today, clipped on the side with pink barrettes. Max thought she was adorable.

"I texted you, but there was no answer," Keiko told her.

Max pulled her phone out of her pocket. She'd put it on vibrate when she went to the beach. "You're right on time. Keep it up. That will make Darlene happy."

"Darlene will love me," Keiko said.

"I like your confidence."

"Do you want to hear what I found out?"

"What you found out about what?"

"About our murder suspects, of course."

Max frowned. "I thought we all agreed we would leave the investigating up to the police and stay out of it. It's not safe." It was possible that someone they knew was a murderer, and she didn't think they would like it if someone started getting too close. It was one thing for her to investigate, but she didn't want to involve anyone else.

"I never agreed to any such thing. And don't tell me you haven't been trying to figure out who killed Jennifer. I can see the bags under your eyes. I bet you were up all night thinking about it."

"I have bags under my eyes?"

Keiko shrugged. "Besides, what is safer than searching for information on the internet? If we find out anything, we can tell the police. I know Andy is one of your very best friends and I want to help you clear his name."

Max sighed. "Okay, what did you find out?"

Keiko pulled her laptop out of her bag and opened it up on the coffee table. Once she started it up, she read Max her notes.

"Okay, first Andy. He met Stacy at Humboldt State. He was pre-med, but when he got his BS, his GPA was only 2.7. Which is not quite good enough to get into med school."

"Interesting," Max murmured but felt a little guilty listening to details of his personal life he hadn't chosen to share with her.

"Did you know Andy is rich? Or at least his parents are. They own a lot of real estate."

"I know. They own most of this block, including this shop. They don't act like they're rich, though. They're just nice, hard-working people."

"Next, Stacy. She was at school to become a nurse, but I suspect she was looking for a husband. As soon as she and Andy got engaged, she dropped out of school. *Her* GPA was 3.7. She's from a small town called Banquette about 30 minutes outside of Corpus Christi."

"Hmmm. She always said she came from Corpus Christi. She probably just doesn't want to have to explain to everyone where Banquette was. Who else have you been researching?"

"Chad. He lists his address as Jennifer's house, so I guess he has been living with her." Keiko read from her notes on the computer. "Before that, he lived in a house on Aster Street with two other guys. And before that, he lived in Van Nuys with his girlfriend and worked in construction. He plays with the band four nights a week at the Crazy Fox, and he just went to work for RG Distributors. I think he's in sales. And he drives a Mercedes S500 which costs around $100,000."

"Wow!" Max said.

"It's in his name too. I figure Jennifer must have bought it for him."

"You found out all this on the Internet?"

"You would be surprised what you can find out if you are resourceful." Keiko seemed very pleased with herself.

"Legally, right?"

"Max!" Keiko sounded indignant. "You don't think I would do anything illegal, do you?"

"No, of course not." Max was more and more impressed with her young assistant, though she also realized Keiko didn't actually answer the question.

"Anyway, last, and in this case, least, is William Chase, Jennifer's ex-husband."

"How do you know about him?" Max asked.

"Someone mentioned him last night, and I saw him in her contact list on her phone. I took pictures of it last night. I also took a picture of her schedule from the day she died. The police are assuming the cake killed her, but maybe it was something she ate or drank earlier in the day. I figured it would help to know where she went."

So that's what Keiko was doing with the phone last night.

"Okay, so why do you say William Chase is last and least?"

"Even though they were only married for three years, she got a lot of money in the divorce settlement plus the house she lived in and the Crystal Shores Playhouse. He moved to New York, got remarried, and has a three-year-old child with his new wife."

"He doesn't seem like a likely suspect," Max noted.

"True. It seems as if he has moved on. And as far as I could tell, he's not in town."

"I'm not going to get anywhere without a motive. Plenty of people disliked her or even hated her, but enough to kill her? And why now? That's the question I keep asking myself."

"Yes," Keiko agreed. "That is a very good question." The shop phone started to ring.

"A question I can't come up with an answer for." Max thought out loud as Keiko rushed to pick up the phone.

"Wedding Belles Bridal, how may I assist you? Yes, she's right here." She handed the phone to Max. "It's Fiona."

Fiona asked if she'd like to go along to visit Jennifer's mother. Max wasn't sure why Fiona wanted her to go along, but she agreed, and they made plans for three o'clock. She was curious to meet the woman who raised Jennifer, and she hoped she'd be able to sneak in a few questions. She'd always thought it was a little odd that Jennifer's mother had never come to the shop with her daughter for any of the consultations or fittings. Max asked Keiko if she would be okay if she left her by herself for a while that afternoon. Keiko just made a face, which Max took to mean yes. Then she went to the office to put her things away.

The door jingled and Curtis came in with a small package.

"Hi, Curtis. Where's this one from?" She waited for a reply. "Curtis?"

Keiko had come out from the office.

"Hi!" Curtis said.

"Oh, this is Keiko. She just started working with us yesterday. Keiko, this is Curtis. He brings us many beautiful things from faraway lands."

"Pleased to meet you, Keiko."

The two young people stared at each other. Or at least Curtis stared. Keiko's look was more of a glare.

"I hope you don't mind me saying so, but you're very *kawaii*."

"*Kawaii?*" Max asked. Keiko didn't respond.

"It means cute or adorable," Curtis told her. "At least, that's what I think it means. Keiko could probably explain it better than me."

Awkward silence. Max decided to break it.

"So... you have a package for me?"

"Oh, yes. Sorry, yes, you have a package. From New York. It's quite heavy for a small package."

"It must be the buttons I ordered. We go through a lot of buttons around here. You know, for the wedding gowns?" Curtis seemed to be in a trance as if he couldn't take his eyes off Keiko. "Hello?"

"Sorry, yes. Buttons. Well, I'd better be going. Nice to meet you, Keiko."

Keiko said nothing as he left.

"You weren't very nice to Curtis," Max told her.

"He was staring at me," she said, scowling.

"Well, you are very cute. Or should I say *kawaii?*"

"What does he know about *kawaii?*" Keiko grumbled.

"Curtis is a very nice young man. You could at least be polite."

"Fine," she said grudgingly.

"Sorry." Keiko's behavior puzzled Max. "Apparently, I just turned into my mother. But he really is nice, and funny. And he's obviously taken with you. I don't see what's so wrong with him."

Keiko stood with her arms folded.

"Okay, you're right. It's none of my business. Just please at least be polite."

They were interrupted by Tiffany's arrival. A stunning young woman, Max guessed her to be in her mid to late twenties. She wore a long black dress, heavy mascara, and her hair was dyed dark blue. Max invited her to sit down and offered her something to drink. Keiko brought them both bottled water and went back to the office to finish the filing project she had started.

"I just want to get straight to it," Tiffany said. "I don't know if you can help, but you seemed like my best shot. I've read your reviews online."

"Okay, I'll skip the small talk," Max replied. "What do you have in mind?"

"My fiancé wants me to wear a wedding dress to our wedding. His family is all going to be there, and he wants a more traditional wedding than I would want. He knows if I had my way, my wedding dress would be black, but he's begging me to wear a white dress. Or at least off-white. He said 80%."

"He actually said 80%?"

"I negotiated him down from 90%. How I wound up falling in love with an accountant, I'll never be able to explain, but I love him so much that I've agreed to the big wedding he wants. Or at least his family wants. I want to make him happy, but bridal gowns all look the same to me. All girly or fluffy. I don't want to look like Cinderella or even Princess Kate. I've been through all the magazines, and I can't imagine wearing any of the dresses I've seen."

"What do you envision?"

"That's just it. I don't know. In my mind, I imagine a work of art. Something unique and creative. Like something Galadriel would wear."

"Galadriel?"

"She's the elfin queen in *Lord of the Rings*. Cate Blanchett played her in the movies."

"Oh, of course. I read all the books in high school." Max had an idea. "Excuse me a moment."

Max stuck her head in the office and asked Keiko if she could borrow her sketchbook. Keiko raised her eyebrows but gave Max the book.

Max paged through until she came to the right drawing.

"What do you think of this dress?" she asked Tiffany, showing Keiko's drawing of a dress with a leather corset and a long billowing skirt.

"Yes!" Tiffany beamed. "This is amazing! I didn't know you designed dresses like this."

"I don't," Max admitted. "Let me get the designer."

Max brought Keiko from the office and introduced the two women. When Keiko realized what was going on, she asked to speak with Max alone.

"Oh no, this is not good. I cannot make that dress. I'm still learning pattern making. I've never made anything like it."

"But I can help you make it," Max assured her. "If you'll let me. I'll want you involved at every step of the way, but I can see it in my head. I know just what fabrics to use. I just need to find the leather, and I bet you can help with that."

"That would be wonderful! To have one of my designs actually created and worn by someone. And on her wedding day. It would be a dream come true for me."

"I told you dreams happen in this shop."

As soon as Tiffany left, they started brainstorming ideas for the dress, which made Max very hungry. She offered to pick up sandwiches for both of them, but Keiko said she had plans. Max sat down to think about which of her favorite places she wanted to go for lunch, while Keiko got on the computer in the office to research leather suppliers.

A woman entered the shop. Max guessed her to be in her mid-fifties and she wore her mousy brown hair in a short, practical hairstyle. Well, brides come in all shapes and sizes.

"Hi, I'm Sharon," the woman said, reaching out her hand to shake Max's. "I'm here to pick up Kathy."

"Kathy?"

Just then, Keiko came out of the office. "Hi, Mom. I see you met Max."

"Kathy?" Max repeated.

"Mom, please. At least with other people, can you quit calling me that?"

"I'm sorry, sweetheart. It's hard for me to get used to. I keep thinking you'll grow out of it."

"I've been Keiko for two years, Mom. I changed my name legally. This is not some kind of a phase." She sighed. "Come on, let's go to lunch."

Well, that was unexpected. Keiko hadn't talked much about her family, only saying she was raised by a single mom and her father lived in Japan. It seemed that her new assistant was more interesting than she originally thought.

And it turned out her day would soon get even more interesting.

CHAPTER 10

*M*ax was in the workroom when she heard the doorbell jingle. She came into the showroom and found Detective Cruz there.

"Are you busy?" he asked.

They sat down in the showroom and Max wondered what other questions he had for her. She'd already told him everything she knew. The detective seemed nervous or uncomfortable. She couldn't figure out which. Or why.

"I know you think Andy is not guilty," he began.

"I know he's not guilty," she interrupted.

"Let me finish, please." He took a deep breath and continued. "There was so much pressure to make an arrest, from the public and from the mayor. And all the evidence points to Andy. I shouldn't be telling you this, but it was the Police Chief's decision to arrest Andy. I wanted to wait for the report on the cake samples. But, in spite of that, I'm sure we have our murderer."

"Did you even investigate anyone else?" she asked.

"Honestly, I feel like I've investigated everyone. Officially, the investigation is closed."

"Officially?" she asked.

"Let's just say I'm keeping my eyes and ears open."

"So, you're not completely convinced that Andy's guilty."

"I'm not saying that. We have the right guy." It was like Detective Cruz was trying to tell her something without actually telling her.

"Then why are you here?"

"I wanted to tell you how sorry I am. I imagine you hate me right now for arresting your friend. I know this is hard for you."

"I don't hate you." At least she didn't think she did. "I am pretty angry. What evidence do you have that makes you think that Andy killed Jennifer?"

"Trust me. We have evidence."

"You don't know him. He's a really good guy." Max told him stories about Andy growing up, about how he volunteered at the local animal shelter, and how he put off college to help run the bakery when his dad had wrist surgery. While other kids were off partying, he went to bed early so he could get up at 4:30 and help his mom bake bread and pastries. She left out the part about her falling in love with him. She didn't realize how long they'd been talking until Keiko returned. Keiko stopped when she entered the shop and didn't say anything, but just stood there for a moment, then passed by them and went in the office.

"I'd better run," Detective Cruz said, rising from his

chair. "Can we keep this conversation between the two of us?"

"As long as you promise to keep an open mind."

Cruz nodded. "Take care, Max."

She watched him leave. Maybe there was hope for him yet.

After he left, Keiko came out of the office. "What did he want?"

"I'm not sure. I think he just wanted to apologize for arresting Andy." And hint to her that he wasn't convinced that Andy was guilty? Her stomach grumbled. She told Keiko she was going to run out to get a bite.

"I brought you some lentil soup from the Cheshire Cat," Keiko said, handing her a bag. "I thought you might not get a chance to get away. It's quite delicious."

"I love their lentil soup! Thank you, Keiko. Let me give you some money."

"No, please, let it be my treat."

"Thanks!" She took the soup back to the workroom. When she finished with her soup, she went back to work on the alterations while Keiko watched the shop and answered the phone. Fiona stopped by right at three o'clock. Max reminded Keiko all she needed to do while she was gone was to let people know she would be back in an hour. Max and Fiona walked out back and got in Fiona's red 2001 Jaguar S-Type.

"Nice car," Max commented. "Isn't Teresa going with us?"

"Teresa said she wanted to reorganize the shop. I think the real reason she didn't want to come is that

119

she doesn't like Sonia. Teresa says she's a floozy. She said that after she saw her talking to one of the men at the senior center that Teresa had her eye on. She's afraid he'll go after Sonia because she's younger."

"I thought once you got to your sixties, you'd quit fighting over boys."

"Teresa's 72. But she can be just as jealous as a sixteen-year-old."

Fiona pulled out of the parking space and drove down the alley. She took two sharp turns while Max held on to the armrest. They drove on Coast Highway past the old movie theater. Fiona explained the movie theater had been designated as a historic building, so they wouldn't be tearing it down after all. Fiona sat on the committee that had worked to get the designation, and now they were raising funds for the renovation. They had planned to work on getting historic status for the Crystal Shores Theater next. They thought they had plenty of time until Jennifer started talking about tearing it down.

"I guess we'll have more time now," Fiona said. "I wish it were under different circumstances. I never liked the woman, but I never would have wished her dead."

"It'll take some time to settle her estate, I would imagine. I assume Jennifer's mother will inherit everything, don't you think?"

"I hadn't really thought about it," Fiona answered. "I suppose she will. I guess that means we'll be brown-nosing her to keep the theater open."

"Oh, Fiona," Max laughed.

"I'm just being practical."

Fiona turned left at Amaryllis, a little faster than Max would have liked, drove two blocks and pulled up in front of a nondescript stucco home.

The lawn needed mowing and there were brown patches. There was a drought, so maybe Sonia was conserving water. They walked up to the cement porch, which was flanked by small, neglected shrubs. Fiona knocked on Sonia's front door, and a mature woman opened the door. She appeared to be around sixty but trying hard to look forty. Her medium-length, frosted hair was neatly styled, and she wore a low-cut T-shirt and skintight jeans.

Fiona introduced Max, and Sonia invited them in. They stepped onto brown, worn carpet into a small living room. Fiona and Max sat on a beige velour sofa, while Sonia slid into a brown leather recliner that might have been around since the Sixties. Obviously, Jennifer was not supporting her mother in style.

They told her how sorry they were for her loss, and Max felt awkward, not knowing what to say, when Fiona announced, "Max's going to solve her murder."

"I thought they arrested Andy." She reached for a cigarette from the pack on the chrome and glass end table.

"Yes," Max said, "but we don't think he did it."

Sonia grunted. "Neither do I. What does the Crystal Shores police know about finding murderers? They're glorified traffic cops. I've heard about you, Max. They say you've got a sixth sense about finding things. I bet you could find my Jennifer's murderer."

"Well then, if you don't mind," Max said, "can we ask you some questions?"

"You can ask me anything." She picked up a red disposable lighter, clicked it five or six times until it lit, and sucked at her cigarette until the tip glowed. "I don't know if I can tell you anything that will help. I hadn't seen her for six months. I wasn't even invited to the wedding!"

"That's awful!" No wonder she had never come with Jennifer for any of her fittings. Well, she could cross her off her suspect list. "Why not?"

"The first time Jennifer introduced me to Chad, she told me she was going to marry him." She took a long drag off the cigarette. "I told her she was making a big mistake. I told her the only reason he was marrying her was for her money."

The same thought had occurred to Max. "What did she say?"

Sonia balanced the cigarette on the edge of an ashtray full of butts. "She said she never wanted to see me again as long as she lived!" Suddenly, she started to sob. "And she didn't!" she wailed. "I should never have said that to her!"

Fiona gave her a tissue, and Max waited for her to compose herself.

"You don't think he was marrying her for her money?" Max asked.

Sonia scowled at her. "Of course, he was. I just never should have said so."

Max decided to be direct. "Do you think he killed Jennifer?"

"It had to have been him. Jennifer changed her will the morning she died. She told me she was leaving everything to him. You've got to prove he did it, or he'll get everything."

That was interesting information. She wondered if the police knew. Max wondered if Sonia was more upset about Jennifer's death or about not inheriting anything. "Is there anyone else besides Chad who might have wanted, well, harm to come to her?"

"No one. Everyone loved my Jennifer."

"Everyone?" Max asked. Were they talking about the same person?

"Well, except for the people who were jealous." She stared at the smoke rising from the cigarette and spoke as if in a trance. "My Jennifer was beautiful. And the people she worked with were jealous of her success. She sold more homes than anyone at her office. People accused her of stealing clients away or not playing fair, but she was just more aggressive than the others. If a man's aggressive, they say good for him, but if a woman's aggressive, they call her a bitch." She picked up the cigarette, took three angry puffs, and put the cigarette back on edge of the ashtray. Max stared at it nervously, thinking it wouldn't take much for it to fall off and burn the house down.

"Is there anyone in particular who was jealous of her success?" Max asked.

"Oh, everyone at her office." Sonia reached over and took a drink of some brown liquid in a short glass. Max didn't think it was tea.

"Anyone who might have wanted to see her dead?"

"That Nancy woman." Sonia put the drink down. "She had it out for my Jennifer. She couldn't handle the competition. Now that Jennifer's gone, she'll get all her old clients back. That's motive for murder, isn't it?"

"Maybe." It seemed like a bit of a stretch to Max. Her parents had been friends with Nancy Addison and her husband, though she chose not to mention it to Sonia. Nancy had lost her husband recently. Max wondered if her dad still kept in touch with her.

Fiona asked about the funeral and told her they would both be there.

As they walked to the car, Max said, "Why did you tell her I'd be at the funeral? I don't like going to funerals in general, and I especially don't want to go to Jennifer's funeral."

"Max, dear, don't you know anything? The funeral is the perfect place for sleuthing."

"Well, then, I hope the murderer's been caught before then."

They drove back to the shop in silence. Sonia didn't seem like a very nice person, but it didn't seem like she had any motive for murdering her own daughter. Plus, she didn't have opportunity since she hadn't seen her in six months. Then there was Nancy. Max liked Nancy, but she had to keep an open mind.

When she got back to the shop, Keiko was organizing the thread spools by color.

"I hope you don't mind. I wanted to make myself useful. I wanted them to be like they are at the fabric store."

"I don't mind at all. I like it a lot. Let's just hope Darlene likes the new order."

"I thought you did all the sewing."

"Lately, that's true," Max admitted. "But that doesn't mean she won't have an opinion. Anything happen while I was out?"

"River stopped by with the mail," Keiko told her. "I put it on the desk."

"Thanks. Did he have any words of wisdom?"

"Actually, he did." Keiko tried to remember. "Something about muddy water. I think it was if you let it stand it becomes clear. He said to tell you that. Although he said it better."

"He's a wise mailman." Max checked her watch. "I have an appointment for a pedicure if you don't mind watching the shop for a while longer."

"I don't mind at all. Are you going to Salon Fred?"

"Salon Frederique. Yes, actually. I put on sandals this morning and realized my toes need help. I don't normally go out for pedicures in the middle of the workday. Just so you know," Max explained.

"You do not need to explain to me." Keiko kept putting spools in order. "I hope you learn something. Oh, don't pretend with me. I know the real reason you're going. When I finish with this, I think I will go through the dresses so I can get more familiar with them. I read up on the types of dresses, mermaid, ball gown..."

"Trumpet, which is like a modified mermaid. A-line. Empire."

"They're organized by style, right?"

"Right. And if you think you have a better way to organize them, ask me first, please. Otherwise, I won't be able to find anything. Well, I should be back by five. I have my phone and it's actually turned on and charged. Call me if you need anything."

"Good luck." Keiko went back to her thread organizing.

"Thanks!" Max called out as she went out the front door.

She crossed the street and walked south for three blocks to Salon Frederique. She entered the tiny salon.

"Hi, Lani," she said to the owner who stood at the reception desk.

"Hi, Max. Where have you been? How long since I've seen you?"

"Probably since fall when my toes went into hibernation."

"Mai will fix you up good."

"Hi, Mai, how have you been?" Max asked her favorite manicurist.

"Great! Mani-pedi today?"

"Just pedi today. I put on sandals this morning and realized I needed help."

"You need a mani too!" Mai grabbed her hands and investigated her cuticles.

They didn't look that bad, did they? Okay, maybe they did. "All right. Mani, too," she told Mai.

Max sat in the massage chair and adjusted the settings. After what she thought was a suitable amount of small talk, she decided to bring up the subject she really wanted to broach.

"I understand Jennifer was here on Monday," she said.

"Yes, she was wearing those hootchie-mama boots."

"Hootchie-mama?" Max asked.

"Oh, you know. Those boots are for catching a man. She already caught a man. Why did she need them? You should get some boots like hers, Max."

"What?"

"It might help," Lani joined in.

"Might help what?" Max asked.

"Might help you get a man," Lani continued.

"And get one of those push-up bras. Men like those," Mai said.

"They do," Lani added.

"I don't need a man," Max grumbled. There were a number of plusses to being single. Not that she wanted to be single forever. "Although, it might be nice."

"Of course," Mai said. "They can be nice to have around. When they're not being jerks."

"It's true," Lani said. "Sometimes they can be jerks. Not worth the trouble."

"Well, I'm glad that's settled," Max muttered.

"I can't believe Jennifer is dead," Mai said. "I heard it was murder. Is that true?"

"The police think so."

"I wonder who killed her."

"Any ideas?" Max asked.

"She argued with her mother on the phone. But I can't imagine a mother…" Mai didn't finish the thought.

"What were they arguing about?" Max asked.

"She told her she didn't want her coming to the wedding."

"Anything else you remember?"

"She made a bunch of calls. She was always on her phone. She called her office and was very rude to someone. Of course, she was rude to everyone. And there was something else." Mai leaned closer and talked in a hushed voice. "She talked to someone about a secret. She kept saying, don't worry, I won't tell her. Very suspicious."

"That does sound suspicious. Anything else?" Max asked.

"She left a lousy tip. As usual," Mai told her.

"She was cheap," Lani said. "But she did look good."

Max got back to the shop just before five. There wasn't much else to do so she told Keiko she could go on home.

"I'm meeting with Fiona and Teresa, remember? I told them 5:15, but I think I'll head on over so I can check out the store."

"They have some very unique yarns. Fiona has a collection of lovely hand-dyed yarns."

"Do you knit?" Keiko asked.

"No, but my mom did. She said it helped her relax." Max remembered her mom on the living room sofa, knitting while they watched TV together. "Fiona and Teresa have a knitting club that meets every week, and my mom always went. She was always knitting something, but they always came out terribly. Eventually, she realized she should just stick to blankets and simple things like that. I would help her pick out the yarn since she had no sense for color. My dad was always the creative one."

"I know nothing about yarn," Keiko admitted. "But I'm a quick learner. I'll see you in the morning."

"Wait, I'll go with you." Max hadn't been to the yarn shop since her mother passed away, and it was about time she stopped in. "Let me just run the vacuum cleaner."

Ten minutes later, Max and Keiko walked in the front door of The Knitpickers. Nothing seemed to have changed, but Max was struck by the brightly colored yarns that lay in wooden bins on both sides of the wall. Max could almost see her mom sitting at the big wooden table knitting with other ladies in one of Fiona and Teresa's classes.

Teresa came out from the back. "Hello, Keiko. Hello, Max," she said and hugged them both. "Fiona is tallying the day's receipts. I'll show you around while we're waiting for her to finish."

"You have a beautiful shop," Keiko said.

"Thank you. We wanted it to feel homey and warm so people would want to stay for a while." She walked over to one side of the shop and pulled a skein of yarn out of one of the bins. "This is one of our most popular yarns. It's organic cotton and bamboo. We don't carry much in the way of synthetic yarns. Most of our customers prefer cotton or wool. Over here," she led them to a display toward the back of the room, "is our hand-dyed cotton yarn. Fiona dyes them herself."

"The colors are stunning!" Keiko picked up a skein. "And it's so soft."

Max said, "Fiona will even dye to order if you want a particular color they don't carry."

Keiko took a notebook out of her Totoro bag and wrote herself a note. "We definitely want to highlight that on your website. I bet there are people out there who can't find the color they want anywhere."

Teresa was showing them their specialty yarns, like cashmere and silk, when Fiona came out of the back room.

"Welcome to our shop, Keiko," she said. "What do you think?"

"It's a lovely shop. And I'm going to make you a website that has the same homey feel. I brought my camera so I could take pictures. Shall we get to work?"

Max said her goodbyes and stepped out onto the sidewalk. She stood there for a moment, thinking of all the times she had gone to the Knitpickers with her mom, helping her pick out yarn for her next project. Why was it always the little things that made her miss her mother so much?

She looked in at the bakery, but it was dark. She wondered if there was any news about Andy.

 *M*ax walked home, passing neighbors out walking their dogs or power walking for their nightly exercise. She went to her dad's and found him in his workroom, cleaning his brushes.

"I have some bad news. They've charged Andy," he said.

"No! That's terrible. Who told you?"

"Fiona called just now. She wanted to tell you, but she thought it would be better if the news came from me."

Max sat down and put her head in her hands. This couldn't be happening!

"He's got a good lawyer," Richard said. "I bet it doesn't even go to trial."

"But what if it does? What if Andy has to sit through a long trial with a jury sitting there staring at him like he's some sort of monster? And what if he gets convicted?"

Richard tried to reassure her, but nothing he said made her feel better.

"I made stew for dinner, but now I'm not hungry," she said.

"I was going to invite you to come to dinner with Nancy and me, but if you're not hungry..."

"Nancy? That's funny, I was just wondering if you two were still in touch. Sonia mentioned her." Max wanted to ask if they were dating, but then again, she didn't really want to know.

"Why don't you join us?" he asked. "We can walk there together. It's a nice night for a walk. Maybe it will help get your mind off things."

"If I'm not going to be in the way." She had an ulterior motive for wanting to go, and it had nothing to do with getting her mind off of Andy or the murder.

"Nonsense. I'm sure she'd love to see you."

Considering what Sonia had said about Nancy, Max thought she'd like the opportunity to ask a few questions. She'd have to be sneaky about it, which was not one of her strong suits. Besides, maybe she could tell if Nancy had designs on her dad.

They met Nancy at The Clay Pot, an Indian restaurant a block from the Crazy Fox. They ordered tandoori chicken, spinach, rice and the wonderful flat Indian bread called naan. Nancy and Richard talked about painting, the weather, and Nancy's daughter, who was in college. Max didn't know how to bring up the subject of Jennifer and the murder with her dad there, but she needn't have worried. It was the subject of everyone's conversation these past couple of days.

"I didn't kill her, but I have to say I'm not going to shed any tears because she's gone," Nancy told them.

"Did you two have a falling out?" Max took a bite of chicken.

"I'll say! I left my old company to come to Crystal Shores Realtors a couple of years ago, and I brought my client base with me. Jennifer used to take me out, buy me dinner, and ask me for advice. She seemed so sincere. She asked me about my clients, and like a stupid idiot, I told her about them. Next thing I know, I've lost three of my clients. Guess who their new agent was?"

"Jennifer?"

"Jennifer. One listing was a four-million-dollar home. That's one big commission. I've got a daughter at SC. Do you know how much it costs to go to SC?"

"A lot?" Max guessed.

"You bet! As far as I'm concerned, that's no different than stealing. She stole from me, and what's worse, she pretended to be my friend. I might have poisoned her myself if I'd thought of it."

Max tried to remember if she'd mentioned Jennifer had been poisoned. Then again, it didn't seem like anything remained a secret in this town. She asked a few more questions, but Nancy had avoided Jennifer for the past year, so she didn't have much information.

"Did you see her the day she died?" Max asked. She hoped she didn't sound obvious like she was asking for an alibi.

"I saw her that morning. She stopped by to pick up some paperwork. I was there the rest of the day, and I didn't see her after that. She kind of made her own hours. I don't know why she got away with it."

Richard and Nancy talked about other things through the rest of dinner, while Max's mind wandered. Nancy didn't seem like a killer, but then, she wasn't sure what a killer seemed like.

In the books she read, killers were sometimes unlikeable people who you were happy to see arrested at the end. But in other books, the murderers seemed like normal people who were nice to your face until they were cornered. Would she be able to tell if someone she knew were a killer?

Richard paid the tab, ignoring Nancy's offer to contribute. They stepped outside into the dark night and said their goodnights. Max and Richard walked down Coast Highway in silence until Richard spoke up.

"I didn't know Nancy was on your suspect list when I invited you to join us."

"What?" Max tried to feign innocence and then decided to fess up. "Sonia thinks she had a motive." She felt bad about suspecting one of her dad's friends. "I'm sorry. I know the two of you go way back."

"I don't think she did it," he told her as they turned down Rose Street. There were no streetlights on their street, but the full moon lit their way.

"I don't think so either. Even if she were capable of murder, why would she wait until now to do it? Plus, she was pretty open about how much she didn't like Jennifer. She's not acting like I would think a guilty person would act." How that was, she wasn't sure. Still, she wasn't going to cross Nancy off her suspect list just yet. Her dad didn't need to know that.

"And she only saw her in the morning," Richard added.

"I wish we knew when she had been poisoned. I wonder if the police know. Maybe they have an autopsy report by now."

"What happened to letting the police handle it?" Richard asked.

"I can't help it, Dad. My mind keeps trying to put all the pieces together. And now that Andy's been charged, the police will have stopped considering any other suspects. I just want to help."

"And I don't suppose anything I say is going to stop you from trying to figure it out."

"I'm being careful. I promise."

"I'm just afraid you're going to question the wrong person. Remember, someone is a murderer. If they figure out you're on to them..."

"I get your point." She wanted to reassure him, but she didn't want to lie to him either.

"It's only a quarter to eight. Casablanca is playing at the Century. Wanna go?"

The Century started playing classic movies every Wednesday night around the time she came back from New York, and she went with her parents nearly every week until her mom got too sick to go.

"We haven't gone for a while," Max said.

"I don't think you and I have ever gone without your mom. Are you up for it?"

Max smiled. She'd never stop missing her mom, but it was time to make new memories with her dad. "I'd love to," she said, putting her arm through his.

"Here's lookin' at you kid," Richard said, and they quoted lines from the movies until they got to the box office.

It was after ten when Max said goodnight and went up the stairs to her apartment. She put on pajamas and curled up on the sofa. She turned on the TV and flipped through all the channels to see if there was something to get her mind off the murder. She was tired of thinking about it, but she couldn't stop.

She got up and poured herself a glass of white wine. Then she sat down at the kitchen table with her laptop. She started researching cyanide poisoning but didn't learn anything that would help her figure out when Jennifer had been poisoned. Apparently, how quickly it acted depended on the dose.

She stared at the computer screen with her mind wandering when there was a knock at the door. She closed the laptop and opened the door to find Eric there. He accepted a glass of wine and sat down on her sofa. After squirming a bit in his seat, he got up and dug under the sofa cushions, pulling out a hairbrush. He shook his head as if to say "Really?"

"There's my brush! I have been wondering where it was."

"Max, I love you, but you would lose your head if it wasn't attached. You're always so forgetful." He sat back down and took a sip of wine. "Why are you always finding things for other people, but not for yourself?"

"I wish I knew. I've wondered that myself." She sat down next to him. "Didn't you have a date tonight?"

"Yes, and I'm here and it's 10:45. What does that tell you?"

"You're learning restraint in your old age?" she asked.

"The day I learn restraint is the day you can put me in an old age home. If we were hitting it off, I'd be out until at least midnight. If we were *really* hitting it off, well, who knows."

"Oh. Sorry."

"I think everyone who knows two gay people think they must be perfect for each other because they're both gay. It helps if they have something in common. Jonathan is a banker. He likes to golf. Golf--yuck!"

Eric filled her in on all the details of his dinner. She thought he spent a lot of time talking about someone he wasn't interested in.

"Enough about my non-existent love life." He took another sip of his wine. "What kind of wine is this? It's not your usual cheap stuff."

It wasn't her usual cheap stuff. It was different cheap stuff. "Okay, we'll change the subject. Why don't you tell me why you lied to the police about seeing Jennifer the day she died?"

"It wasn't important, so I just decided not to mention it."

Max crossed her arms. "Tell me. What happened?"

Eric sighed. "I can never get anything past you. We had a huge fight, and she fired me."

"What did you fight about?"

"She wanted to change her order again. She refused to take my advice and told me she had more talent as a floral designer than I did. I told her she could go to hell. Then she fired me."

"You need to tell Detective Cruz."

"It doesn't have anything to do with the murder, so he doesn't need to know."

"But if he finds out, you'll seem guilty."

"Max, the only way he's going to find out is if you tell him. And you're not going to tell him. Right?"

Max hesitated. "I'm sorry, Eric, but if you don't tell him, I will. If he finds out I'm keeping things from him, there's no way I'm going to get him to keep me in the loop."

He frowned. "You're such a rule follower." He finished the last of his wine. "Fine, I'll call him tomorrow." He moaned as he stood up to go.

"What's wrong with you?"

"I worked out with a new trainer at the gym. He gave me quite a workout."

"I was thinking of going to the gym," Max said.

"You?" he laughed. After she gave him one of her famous glares, he added, "What a great idea. The guy I saw today was really good. His name is David West."

"Where do I know that name?" Max thought out loud. "I know. That's Susan Brown's fiancé! What did you think of him? Is he a nice guy?"

"Max, it was a workout, not a social meeting." He took another sip of wine. "I did find out he was Jennifer's personal trainer."

"I remember she said she got a new trainer."

"He said he had been working with her for about five or six weeks. He said they didn't talk much, and he didn't know much about her." He paused, smirking at her. "I just thought you might like to know in case you were looking into the murder."

"I'm just trying to find the real murderer and clear Andy's name," she said. "I hate to think of him in jail, even for a day. But what you've told me so far isn't much help."

"I'm not done. He went on to say he didn't think she had any friends. He said she brought in Chad's sister Kelly and paid for a training session for her. Kelly was going to be her Maid of Honor, and Jennifer wanted her to lose weight."

"I met Kelly," Max said. "Jennifer wanted me to order a size eight for her bridesmaid dress since she said Kelly would be a size smaller by the wedding. I ordered a ten anyway."

"Kelly wasn't interested in losing weight. She liked the way she looked. David said their relationship seemed strained."

"Maybe I can ask Keiko to look her up on the Internet. And Nancy Addison." Max walked Eric to the door.

"From the real estate office?"

"Yeah. She seems pretty angry."

"Angry enough to kill?"

"Good question. But even if she were, why now? Jennifer stole a bunch of clients from her, but that was a couple of years ago." Max was thoughtful. "Keiko has been a big help looking things up. She can find almost anything online. Do you think she might be a hacker?"

"She did major in computers before, didn't she? What makes you think she's a hacker?"

"She just seems good at finding out things about people. Which makes her really useful."

"You really are serious about investigating this murder, aren't you?" Eric asked.

"Just don't tell my dad."

"Oh, you won't keep my secret, but you expect me to keep yours?" Eric put his hands on his hips.

"I just don't want him to worry." She realized she had something she needed to tell Eric. "Before you go, I have some news. I'm moving back to New York to be an assistant designer for Bissette."

"That's fantastic!" he said with a big smile.

"Aren't you going to miss me?" Max asked, a little disappointed that he was so enthusiastic about her leaving.

"Are you kidding? I'll be coming to New York at least twice a year to see you. We'll go to Broadway plays, go to all the fancy restaurants."

"It pays pretty well, but I'm not sure I'll be able to afford fancy restaurants."

"The shop's doing great. It'll be my treat. You just have to let me sleep on your sofa, so I don't have to rent a hotel room."

"Sounds great."

After Eric left, she wondered if he really would call Detective Cruz tomorrow. And what would the detective think about Eric lying to him? Hopefully, he wouldn't be in too much hot water.

CHAPTER 12

The sound of raindrops against her windows woke Max up shortly before her alarm. She wouldn't be walking to work today. At least she hoped she wouldn't. She should probably try to remember where she'd left her umbrella.

She spritzed her hair with a water bottle and scrunched it while using the diffuser attachment on her blow dryer. No point in straightening or curling her hair when it rained. Not that she spent much time styling her hair when it didn't rain. But she liked having an excuse.

She put on a black pencil skirt and knee-high black leather boots. Not quite hootchie-mama boots, but she liked them. She picked out a green cardigan and threw it on over a black camisole. She pulled on her tan trench coat, pulled the hood over her head, and headed for her dad's back door.

With a belly full of oatmeal and the keys to her

dad's Mini Cooper in her hands, she was on her way. She parked behind the shop and unlocked the back door. After putting her purse away, she checked her schedule. No appointments. She planned to order Susan's gown today. She might be able to finish her alterations if she didn't have any drop-ins.

She walked to the front door to unlock it and turn the sign around and almost stepped on a piece of paper. She picked it up and gasped when she read what it said.

Stop investigating or you'll be next.

She dropped it and tried to think what she should do. Call the police. It must have been the murderer who left it. She didn't want to die.

Why was she not moving? She was aware of banging on the door. Keiko was standing outside waiting to get in. She grabbed a tissue, picked up the paper, put it on the coffee table and opened the door.

"What is the matter?" Keiko asked. "You look like you've seen a ghost."

"There was a letter. Someone must have shoved it under the door," Max said. Keiko walked toward the coffee table. "Don't touch it."

Keiko read the note without picking it up. "Well, that is not good."

Talk about understatements.

Fifteen minutes later, Detective Cruz arrived to pick up the note. He asked her questions about it, but she had little to tell him. He said he doubted there would be fingerprints besides hers, but they'd check anyway.

"I hope you take this threat seriously and stop investigating," the detective warned her.

That sounded like a good idea right now. "Who says I'm investigating?"

"Apparently, the murderer thinks you are. And I know you've been asking questions. Who have you been talking to in the last couple of days?"

"Just my friends. We did go to pay our respects to Jennifer's mom yesterday. And we had dinner with Nancy Addison. She's a friend of my dad's. She's pretty angry about Jennifer stealing her clients." She didn't mention Eric in case he hadn't called yet.

He crossed his arms and stared at her sternly. "I see. Well, I recommend you stay close to home until we've solved this case."

After he left, she tried to make sense out of the jumble of thoughts running around in her mind. Was she in danger? Did this mean she was getting close? She didn't feel like she was any closer than when she started. Did the murderer think she was getting close?

Maybe she should listen to Detective Cruz. She knew he wasn't officially investigating anyone else, but Max had a feeling he wasn't convinced that Andy was guilty. He was probably still investigating without telling his boss, the chief, but was he getting anywhere?

Would Andy spend the rest of his life in jail? The thought of it made her sick to her stomach, but was she really helping? Maybe all her investigating wasn't going to do him a bit of good anyway.

But she had to try. She would just be more careful. She would buy some pepper spray and make sure she locked her door when she got home. If you didn't do what you knew was the right thing every time you got a death threat, then what kind of person were you? She was pretty sure she wasn't making any sense even to herself, but she knew the right thing to do.

Max took a deep breath and saw Keiko as if for the first time. She had two buns on top of her head that looked like mouse ears. She wore a tutu with a t-shirt. The t-shirt had a cat on it with Japanese writing above the picture. She smiled in spite of herself.

"I'm not sure Darlene is going to be a fan of your style," Max told her, standing up. Enough of this sitting around. They had work to do.

"Why do you say such a thing?" Keiko asked.

"Really? You don't think you dress a little, well, differently?"

"I know I do. It's who I am," Keiko said proudly. "I am a Harajuku girl."

"A what?" Max felt old and out of touch.

"Well, I'm not actually a Harajuku girl, since I don't live in Japan. But I'm inspired by them. Harajuku is a part of Tokyo where many young people experiment with fashion. Gwen Stefani has backup singers she calls Harajuku girls. They dress very creatively."

"Darlene's just a little more conventional in her thinking. I tell you what, you can wear whatever you want this week, and then next week, maybe you can tone it down a little."

"Okay, but if I'm going to tone it down, can we talk about you maybe toning it up a little?"

"What are you talking about?" Max thought she looked nice today. She loved wearing her boots.

"You're not a banker, you're a designer," Keiko told her. "And tomorrow, I want you to dress like one," Keiko ordered. "You must have something other than black pants and black skirts in your closet."

"I'm not sure I do, but I'll check." She supposed she might have gotten in a bit of a rut with her style, but she thought her style was classic. In New York, everyone wore black. But she wasn't in New York now, so maybe a little color wouldn't hurt.

Max loved working with Keiko. She hadn't felt this inspired in a while, and she knew Keiko's ideas and creativity made her feel that way. She once felt that passionate about fashion. Plus, she could tell Keiko would challenge her, and she had a feeling that was a good thing. Heck, she was already questioning her wardrobe choices.

She wished she could take Keiko with her to New York. Still, there would be plenty of challenges once she got to New York and all kinds of inspiration. And she would be a real designer.

"I was up half the night on the computer," Keiko told her. "I decided to look up everyone else online, besides the suspects. Boy, you are boring."

"You checked me out online?"

"I figured you were a potential suspect. I mean, you were the only one with her when she died, after all."

Max gasped. "You think I killed her?"

"No, of course not! That's not what I meant!" Keiko reassured her. "I wanted to see things the way the police are seeing it. Get the big picture, you know? I even looked up Fiona and Teresa. They're more interesting than you'd think. Did you know they are Canadian?"

"Yes. Actually, Fiona is an American citizen. She married an American about thirty or forty years ago, but he passed away several years ago. Teresa only stays six months at a time. That's all she's allowed to stay. She seems sad when she has to go back to Canada. I don't think she has anyone there, really."

"That is kind of sad."

"I know." Max remembered what she wanted to ask. "That reminds me. I need you to check out Kelly Alexander and Nancy Addison. If you don't mind?"

"Of course, I will be happy to. Are they suspects?"

"Maybe. See if there's anything you can find. When you have the time. Now, I need to do some training with you. I want you to be up to speed by the time Darlene gets back."

Just then, Curtis arrived with a package.

"Hi, Max. Hi, Keiko."

"Hi, Curtis," Max said and looked at Keiko.

"Hi, Curtis," she mumbled.

"Oh! *My Neighbor Totoro*!" he exclaimed.

Keiko's bag lay on the chair where she'd tossed it when she walked in.

"I love Miyazaki," he continued. "Is that your favorite one of his films?"

"I like *Spirited Away* best," Keiko said shyly.

"That's awesome too," Curtis agreed. "But kinda creepy. When I was a kid, it scared me."

"I never saw it when I was a kid," Keiko told him. "My mom gave me Disney movies to watch."

"Well, Disney's great too, especially when you're a kid. But my parents love to watch all kinds of foreign films. They got me hooked on anime. I love it!"

"Me, too!" Keiko was actually smiling at him.

"Well, I've got to run," Curtis said with a big grin on his face.

After he left, Max said, "Now that wasn't hard, was it."

"If only he were Japanese," Keiko said.

"Oh, now I see. Still, I'm glad you were nice to him."

Keiko rolled her eyes.

Max usually didn't pry, but her curiosity got the better of her. "Why do you only like Japanese guys? You're only half Japanese."

"I just love everything Japanese." She started to play with the lace on her tutu. "My mom raised me, and I was never around anyone or anything Japanese. I never felt like I fit in because of how I look. Then when I went to college, I joined the Japanese club and learned all about the history and culture. And I hung out with kids who looked like me. For once, I felt like I belonged."

"I see. Well, I can relate to not feeling like you belong."

"You?"

"Yeah, I was kind of weird as a kid."

"What do you mean, weird?" Keiko asked.

"Well, for one thing, I preferred watching old black and white movies with my mom to going out to the mall with my girlfriends. Not that I had many girlfriends. I was just kinda shy and awkward."

"You're not that way anymore."

"Thanks, Keiko. I still feel like an awkward teenager a lot of the time."

She started to open the package Curtis had brought her. She loved getting packages. "Some people would say I still am a little weird."

"I would like to see more of that side of you," Keiko said.

"Oh, I'm sure you will, Keiko."

The rest of Max's morning was very productive. She walked Keiko through ordering Susan's gown. Then they made a list of the sample dresses that were outdated and would be offered in the sample sale Darlene did twice a year. The next one was going to be in three weeks.

Max went through the dresses with Keiko, explaining about the different fabrics and trims so she could talk intelligently about them to clients. She stopped mid-sentence and stared out the front door.

"What is it?" Keiko asked, turning.

A black cat was peering in the window. Max could have sworn it looked at both of them, and then it moved on. They went to the door just in time to see the door of The Knitpickers open and the cat saunter in.

"Well, if you were a cat, where would you go?" Keiko asked. "A bridal shop, or a store full of balls of yarn?"

They both laughed. Max went back to explaining about the various dresses. Keiko was doing a very good job paying attention, but Max knew it was time for a break.

Max made a pot of tea and told Keiko to sit down and relax for a few minutes. While the tea was steeping, she brought out two cups and saucers. She was just pouring the tea when Teresa walked in. They both stood up to greet her and Teresa hugged them.

"I like your shirt, Keiko. What a cute kitty cat. What does the writing above the picture say?"

"It says 'nyan nyan'," Keiko said.

"What does nyan mean?"

"It's what cats say in Japan. Instead of meow."

"Japanese cats don't say meow?" Teresa asked.

Keiko smiled and Max started to giggle.

"I guess Japanese people think it sounds more like nyan." Teresa didn't seem convinced.

"Thank you for the tea cozy," Max said. "It's really come in handy. Would you like to join us for tea now?" She motioned to Teresa to sit down and join them.

"Oh, thank you, but I just stopped by to ask a favor of you girls. I need to make some flyers. May I use your printer?"

"Of course," Max answered. "What do you need flyers for?"

"We found a cat. Or it found us. I'm not sure. Her name is Josie."

"We saw the cat through the window. Wait. You know her name?" Max wondered if it had a collar on it.

"Well, no. I'm calling her Josie. She's the sweetest cat. So affectionate. We're going to keep her if we can't find the owner. But of course, I've got to make something of an effort."

"You're welcome to use our printer. Do you want to email me the flyer and I can print it?"

"I haven't actually made a flyer yet," Teresa admitted. "I was hoping you could help me."

"I'll help," Keiko answered. "Do you have a picture?"

"Oh yes. I did that much!" She took out her flip phone and showed Keiko the picture she'd taken.

"Hmm…" Keiko murmured, staring at the phone. "No offense, Teresa, but I can hardly tell that's a cat. Max, can I run next door for a minute? I'd like to take another picture."

Keiko came back with a new picture and had the flyer done in twenty minutes. While the flyers were printing, she offered to stay late to make up for the time she spent working on the side project. Keiko seemed like a very responsible young lady.

Teresa stopped back by to pick up the flyers and went off to post them on telephone poles and signposts around the town.

A few minutes before noon, Olivia arrived for their lunch at Chez Mer.

"Would you like to join us for lunch, Keiko?" Max asked.

"Oh no. Thank you, but I'll stay and watch the shop. I have some errands to run after you get back, if that's okay."

"Yes, of course," Max said.

Max and Olivia stepped out the front door into the bright sunshine. "Should we walk or drive?" Max asked. She looked up and down the street. If someone wanted to hurt her, they wouldn't do it in broad daylight, she was pretty sure of that.

"I think it's done raining," Olivia commented.

"I love it after a rainfall." The fluffy clouds floated by leisurely in the bright blue sky. "It's really beautiful out."

"Then let's walk," Olivia said. "It's only, what, ten blocks or so?" They started walking down the street. "Have you heard anything about Andy?"

"You heard he was charged with murder, didn't you?"

"No, that's awful!"

Let's stop in the bakery and see if there's any news."

The bakery was two doors down from the bridal shop. Stacy stood behind the counter in the empty shop. When she saw them, she ran around to the front and hugged both of them.

"Andy's getting out today," she announced with a smile.

That was great news. "Did they drop the charges?" Max asked.

"No, but he got bail. At least he'll be home. I'm watching the shop while his parents pick him up." She dropped her voice to a whisper. "Have you made any progress finding the real murderer?"

"Nothing yet. I'm retracing her steps from the day she died. We're on our way to Chez Mer where she had lunch that day."

"Well, I've got a clue for you. Know how she always had a bottle of London water with her? The gym where she worked out carries it." She was talking a mile a minute, instead of in her usual slow drawl. "They tried to get us to carry it here, but my in-laws weren't buyin'. I noticed one of our customers had one, and I asked where she got it. Maybe the killer was her trainer or somebody else from the gym. They could have put the poison in the water bottle, and she only drank it hours later."

"That's great information, Stacy. Did you tell the police that?"

"Yes, I called that detective, but he didn't seem interested. You'll look into it, won't you?"

"Sure," Max agreed. "I'll see what I can find out."

A customer came in and Stacy dashed back behind the counter. Max and Olivia said their goodbyes and left. She thought about David West, Jennifer's trainer. Could he be a suspect? But what possible motive would he have?

"So, you have an ulterior motive for going to Chez Mer today?" Olivia asked Max as they continued walking along Coast Highway. "I thought you were just craving a French dip sandwich."

"They do have a fantastic French dip, don't they? But no, I'm checking out all the places Jennifer went on the day she was murdered. She had lunch at Chez Mer that day. I want to find out who she had lunch with."

"She had lunch with Chad," Olivia informed her.

"What?" Max gasped. "How do you know that?"

"I had drinks with her that night."

"You did?"

CHAPTER 13

"I didn't mention having drinks with Jennifer because I know you don't care for her. I mean, didn't."

"I don't have to understand everything you do. I know she was your friend, and I respect that. I'm glad to put together another piece of the puzzle. Two, actually."

"I guess we don't need to have lunch at Chez Mer now," Olivia said.

"Oh yes we do. After talking about it, I really am craving their French dip."

They walked past the hardware store, which had sand chairs and beach umbrellas in the window. Max asked Olivia if they could stop in, and she bought pepper spray. Olivia asked why, and she explained about the note. She tried to reassure her friend that she was fine, but Olivia insisted that Max stay with her. Max said she'd think about it, but she liked sleeping in her own bed. If she didn't feel safe, she could always sleep in her old bedroom at her dad's.

They finally arrived at the restaurant and were seated by the window. Max ordered the French dip sandwich, and Olivia ordered a salad. No wonder Olivia was so slender.

After the server brought their drinks, Max began, "I know you've lost a friend."

"Thanks, but it's not like we were really close. I tried to be friends with her, but it wasn't always easy."

"That's not surprising. Do you mind if I ask what you talked about over drinks?"

"She said she wanted advice about the lighting and staging of the wedding. She wants--I mean--wanted it to be very theatrical." Olivia took a sip of her mineral water. "And I wanted to talk to her about keeping the theater open."

"You said, that's what she *said* she wanted to talk about." Max put a packet of sugar in her tea and stirred it. Of course, most of it settled on the bottom of the glass. Why hadn't they come up with a better way to put sugar in iced tea? "What did she really want to talk about?"

"Chad, of course. Her favorite subject, except, of course, herself. I think she suspected him of cheating on her." The server put a salad in front of Olivia.

"Really?" Max eyed the French dip sitting in front of her. She should try being more like Olivia. "Who did she think he was cheating on her with?"

"I think she thought it was me."

"What?" Max couldn't imagine Olivia cheating with someone else's fiancé. "You?"

"You know how close Chad and I are. Ever since he did *Rent* at our theater, we've spent a lot of time together. We have so much in common. "

"You do?" Max took a bite of her sandwich. It tasted heavenly. The roast beef melted in her mouth. She was so glad she didn't pick today to start being healthy.

"We both love music and musical theater, for one thing." Olivia stabbed her cold salad with her fork.

"Chad loves musical theater?" It surprised Max that he liked anything other than rock and roll. She needed to learn to stop making assumptions about people.

"He's seen *A Chorus Line* ten times. But we don't care for Andrew Lloyd Webber."

"Why not?" How could you not like Andrew Lloyd Webber? The man was a genius.

"I can't talk to you about it," Olivia said. "I know you love Phantom."

"It's true. I do," she admitted. "The question is, why you don't love it?"

"I told you I can't talk about it with you. We have to agree to disagree."

"Fine." Max took another couple of bites of her sandwich before continuing her questioning. "Tell me more about what happened with Jennifer. Did she actually accuse you of having an affair with Chad?"

Olivia shook her head. "No, she was much more subtle. I assured her he wasn't having an affair with anyone, which I truly believe. For some reason, he was totally into her."

"Because of the money?"

"The money helped, but no, I think he actually was in love with her. Sometimes I think love is when one person's neuroses fit with the other person's. Chad and Jennifer fit together, and I think they were actually in love."

Max finished her sandwich and then started in on the French fries. She didn't want to tell Olivia that she suspected Chad of murder. She offered some French fries to Olivia, who said no, of course. "When you had drinks with Jennifer, did you see anyone there who might have had access to her drink? I'm thinking she could have been poisoned before she got to our shop."

"Well, there was the bartender. And there were plenty of other people at the bar." She thought for a moment. "I don't know if any of them could have put poison in her drink without being seen."

"Anyone she knew?"

"Oh, you know Jennifer. Knew." She frowned. "Man, it's hard to get used to talking about someone in the past tense. Anyway, she knew pretty much everyone in town. Celeste was there. She keeps complaining to me about her costumes for *Arsenic and Old Lace*. But then, she complains about every costume in every play. She keeps trying to get Kenneth to fire the costumer."

"And you told me she was upset that Jennifer was planning to close down the theater. Did Celeste say anything to Jennifer?"

"Not a thing. Just fake smiles and air kisses. Watching them, you would have thought they were the best of friends. Except that they didn't actually say a word to each other."

"Did Jennifer talk with anyone else that night?"

"She said hi to a few people. Just casual. Oh, except her mother."

"Her mother?" Sonia had lied to her!

"Yeah, she came over and said she wanted to talk to Jennifer, but Jennifer didn't want to talk to her. She basically told her to get lost."

"That's very interesting. Sonia told me she hadn't seen her in six months."

"Why would she lie?" Olivia asked.

"Maybe she slipped poison in her drink. That would be a reason for her to lie about seeing her." Max thought for a moment. "But she seemed so sincerely upset about Jennifer's death. Maybe she's a good actress. If she was acting, she sure snowed me. What do you think?"

"I don't think a mother could kill her own flesh and blood. Just the thought of it is very disturbing."

"No, you're probably right." Max had second thoughts. "And Jennifer had already changed the will, from what Sonia said. She was leaving everything to Chad. So, I don't see what her motive would be." How disappointing. For a moment, she thought she was on to something.

"Jennifer told her not to come to the wedding."

"That's cold."

"Ice cold. But that's Jennifer."

"Was."

"Oh, right. Was."

They ate the rest of their lunch in silence. Max decided to show restraint and not order dessert. It wasn't that hard because they didn't have anything chocolate on their dessert menu, which seemed ridiculous.

The check came, and for once Max managed to grab it first. After all, she invited Olivia to lunch. If she were a real detective, she would charge lunch to her client. She was starting to feel glad she hadn't decided to become a real detective. When they stepped outside the restaurant, Max looked up and down the street.

"You *are* worried!" Olivia said.

"Just being cautious," Max said, trying to reassure herself as much as her friend.

As they walked, Max resisted the urge to look over her shoulder. She asked Olivia more questions about who might have had access to Jennifer's drink, but Olivia didn't see how someone could have put poison in it in such a crowded bar. The only one who might have had access to the drink was the bartender, and they both agreed he didn't have a motive. Olivia was sure that he and Jennifer barely knew each other.

Back at the shop, they hugged goodbye, and Max went inside. Keiko was waiting for her. "I'm going to run my errand now. I'll be back in a half hour," she said.

"Take your time," Max replied. "If you've got errands to run, you need to eat too. Why don't you take an hour?"

"Great, thanks!"

When Keiko left, Max locked the front door. Hopefully, if anyone stopped by, they would see the open sign and knock, rather than leave thinking the shop was closed.

Shortly after two, Keiko knocked on the door and came in, carrying a small bag. She opened it up and took out two cakes. At least that's what Max thought they were.

"What is this for?" Max asked.

"I am celebrating," Keiko answered. "It is *Shunbun no Hi*."

"It's what?"

"*Shunbun no Hi*. Vernal Equinox Day. It's a national holiday in Japan. It's a day to commune with nature and show our affection for all living things."

"So, cakes? They are cakes, right?" They were quite lovely, frosted in pink and blue.

"Yes. You're a living thing, and how better to show my affection for you than by bringing you a cake. It's from the new Japanese bakery in Fashion Square. I've been meaning to go there, so I figured this was as good an excuse as any."

"Sounds good to me. I'll make a fresh pot of tea."

Max poured them both cups of tea, and Keiko put the little cakes on plates. Max stared at hers and then took a bite. It had some sort of filling that wasn't like anything she'd tasted before. She would have liked to spit it out, but she didn't want to be rude, so she swallowed it in a big gulp.

"Hmmm… Interesting," was all she said.

Keiko frowned. "You hate it. Is it that bad?" She took a bite of her cake and made a face.

"What's the filling?" Max asked.

"It's bean paste."

"Interesting."

"You said that already," Keiko said. She contemplated the rest of the cake sitting on her plate. "They were so pretty." She took both the plates to the bathroom and threw the cakes in the trash.

"Maybe it's an acquired taste," Max suggested. "They really were beautiful."

They were finishing their tea when River opened the door, and they saw a flash of black and white fly by into the office.

"What was that?" he asked.

Teresa dashed in. "Have you seen Josie?"

"I think she went into the office," Max said, and Teresa followed her into the other room.

Max got down on her hands and knees and found the cat under the desk. Its green eyes glared at her. The cat actually looked perturbed.

"What is on her head?" Max asked.

"It's a beret," Teresa told her. "I knitted it."

"You put a hat on a cat?" Max laughed. It sounded so silly. "Unless you're Dr. Seuss, that's just wrong."

"But she looks so cute!"

Max reached for Josie and spotted something else under the desk. It was an empty bottle of water. She left it there and called Detective Cruz.

Twenty minutes later, Keiko poked her head in the workroom. "The detective is here," she told her. "I'll be in here if you need me." Keiko started to make herself appear busy. Apparently, the detective made her nervous.

"Detective Cruz," Max said, greeting him in what she hoped was a warm manner. "I found the bottle of London water. I mean, it must be the bottle. You know, the bottle Jennifer was drinking the night she died. I heard she gets it at her gym."

Why did she always ramble on when she talked to him? It was just because cops made her nervous. Not because she wanted to kiss him. No! Why did she just think that?

Max showed him to the bottle, and he retrieved it and put it in an evidence bag.

"It's convenient the bottle just happened to show up after we already searched the shop," he said suspiciously.

"What are you saying?" Did he think she had something to do with it? "Do you think I put it there? Did your team even check under the desk?"

"Hopefully, we'll get some fingerprints, but I doubt it." Was he deliberately not answering her question? "I'm sure you'd do just about anything to clear your friend's name," he said, which sounded like an accusation, but there was kindness in his voice.

"No, I wouldn't," she snapped. "I would not plant evidence. I would not interfere with a police investigation."

"I hope you've quit going around asking questions." He sounded serious now. "We know who killed Jennifer. You can stop investigating."

"I see my friends. We talk about what we know. Sometimes, yes, I ask questions. Do you expect me to become a hermit and quit talking to everyone?"

"No, of course not. I don't know who wrote that note or why. Maybe it was just meant to scare you. Or maybe someone's trying to throw us off the track. But I'm worried that you could be in real danger. I don't want anything to happen to you."

"I can take care of myself," Max told him.

He put his hands on his hips. "Are you always this frustrating?"

"Sometimes more." Max began to fidget as he stared at her. "Did you know that Chad is going to inherit everything?"

"We know about the will. I would venture to say that I know more than you do, even if you have known these people longer than I have. We've already solved the murder. You're only making it more difficult on yourself by not accepting the truth."

"The truth?" He was so frustrating. "Andy may be charged with murder, but there's no way he's going to be convicted. There are plenty of other people who wanted her dead."

"We are aware she wasn't well liked. We've interviewed many people who are not sad she's dead, but none of them have motive and opportunity."

"But there must be someone else. I've known Andy my whole life. I just don't believe he could do something like this."

"If you keep asking questions, you may find out something you don't want to know," the detective said.

"I want the truth. I don't care what I find out. I won't stop asking questions until I know what really happened." If she found out more than what she wanted to know, she would deal with it. The important thing was that Andy not go to jail for a murder he didn't commit.

"Fine." Detective Cruz paused as if he were deciding what to tell her. "We have evidence that Mr. Fuller and Ms. Burns were having an affair, and she threatened to tell his wife. Now will you stop asking questions?" He waited for her reaction.

"No way Andy was having an affair with Jennifer. That makes no sense. He adored his wife. What so-called evidence do you have that they were sleeping together?"

"Text messages on both their phones. They were deleted, as you might expect, but we retrieved them from their carriers." Detective Cruz sounded smug.

"Oh." Why would Andy have been sending Jennifer text messages? There had to be a logical reason. "Maybe they were texting about the cake."

"The texts did not involve cake. Speaking of cake, we've rushed the tests to find out if there was poison in the cake, so we'll have an answer soon."

"Did you get the autopsy results?" Max asked, deciding on the direct approach. "Do you know how long the poison was in her system before she died?"

"Yes, we got the results." He seemed to be deciding whether to tell her more. "I don't see what it hurts if you know. Based on the amount of poison in her system, we believe she ingested it approximately one to two hours before she died. Since she died shortly after she arrived at the hospital, it's highly likely she was poisoned here, in your shop."

"I see." Max walked over to one of the chairs and sat down. "That's not good. I mean, it's good because it narrows down the suspects, doesn't it? Although she could have been poisoned before she got here. She was only here for maybe half an hour. Let me think." Her mind was a jumble. The poison must have been in the water. "You're going to test the water bottle, aren't you?"

"Of course, we'll test it."

"Andy's not guilty. I've known him all my life. I just know he couldn't do such a thing."

"Max," he began, "I know he's a childhood friend of yours and you think you know him. But people have secrets. Everyone has secrets." He reached over and took her hand. "You need to stay out of it. No more investigating."

After he left Keiko came out from the back room. She had been listening at the doorway, so she'd heard everything. Something had been bugging Max since Detective Cruz had said that the text messages had been deleted.

"What did you do with Jennifer's phone Tuesday night?" Max asked.

"What do you mean?" Keiko sounded so innocent. Too innocent.

It was never a good sign when someone answered a question with a question. Max didn't want to accuse Keiko of anything, but she had to know.

"I mean, what did you do with her phone? It's a simple question." She didn't mean to sound as harsh as her words came out.

"I checked her schedule. I told you. And I took pictures of her contact list."

"And what else?" Max had a feeling she already knew the answer.

"If I tell you, do you promise not to tell him?" Keiko sounded nervous now.

"You mean Detective Cruz? I can't promise anything." Max waited, but Keiko said nothing. "I already know," she bluffed, afraid that she had guessed right. "You deleted text messages off her phone, didn't you?"

"Fine. I saw the text messages to Andy, and they made him look guilty. They were texting back and forth about some kind of secret and how Stacy couldn't find out. I knew he was your friend, so I just deleted them."

"What were you thinking? You could get in so much trouble!"

Keiko's lower lip began to tremble, and Max was afraid she was going to start crying. "I wasn't thinking. There wasn't time to think. I just did it. You won't tell him, will you?"

Max thought about whether it would do anyone any good if she told Cruz that it was Keiko who deleted the texts. "I don't know. I'll have to think about it." She wondered if there was anything else Keiko was hiding from her. "Try to remember exactly what the text messages said."

"I don't remember." Keiko closed her eyes and scrunched her face in concentration. "I think it was 'I want to make sure Stacy doesn't find out. It will ruin everything."

"Anything else?"

Keiko opened her eyes. "I don't remember anything else."

"Okay. Let's think about this logically. What else could Jennifer and Andy be keeping secret from Stacy?"

"I know!" Keiko brightened. "Maybe they were throwing Stacy a surprise party."

Max shook her head. "I don't think that was it. Why would Jennifer help throw a surprise party for Stacy?"

"Fine. Do you have any better ideas?"

"Not right now. I need to think about it."

Max didn't feel like doing any more training. She sat in the showroom paging through the latest issue of Brides magazine, while Keiko worked on her computer in her office. Then she stood staring out the window at the cars going by. A car pulled over, and Andy jumped out of the back seat.

"Andy!" Max called, running out the front door. "I'm so glad you're out."

"You're glad!" He gave her a big hug. "What an awful experience. And it's not over yet."

"Detective Cruz was here a little while ago. He's really frustrating."

"He's just doing his job. Max, you're not trying to find out who murdered Jennifer, are you?"

"Well, someone has to." Max paced back and forth on the sidewalk. "I need to find the real murderer, so they'll drop the charges against you."

He grabbed her by the shoulders. "Max, you need to stop this right away. It's dangerous."

"I won't stop." She felt uncomfortable being so close to him. She could see the worry in his face. "Besides, I'm being careful. I bought pepper spray."

"Pepper spray?" He released her from his grip. "If the murderer thinks you're getting too close, he could come after you, and I don't think pepper spray is going to stop him."

She decided not to tell him about the note. "I have to try. Detective Cruz is stubborn. He's decided you're the killer and he's quit looking at anyone else."

"He's stubborn?" Andy raised his voice. "What about you? I've never known anyone more stubborn in my life! What makes you always think you're smarter than everyone else?"

"What?" Max stared at him in shock. "I do not."

"Yes, you do. You always knew better than me. Stacy thinks I'm smart and capable and can take care of her."

"I think you're smart," Max argued.

They stood there on the sidewalk staring at each other.

Andy gave in first. "Butt out of it! I don't need your help."

Max stared at the man she thought she knew. Did she act like she was smarter than everyone? Or was this Andy's insecurity coming out? She started to wonder how well she knew him. Could he have been involved with Jennifer?

"Andy, I have to ask you. Detective Cruz says you

were having an affair with Jennifer." She paused, not wanting to ask the question. "Were you?"

"No! Of course not! I love my wife and I would never cheat on her. Did you actually think I would?"

"No, I didn't," she said. "But I had to ask. He said there were a bunch of text messages between you and Jennifer."

"I gotta go. Stacy is waiting."

Max wondered why he didn't want to talk about the text messages. Should she press the issue? She decided not to, at least not now. "Go see Stacy. I know she's worried."

"I didn't do it, so there's no reason to worry. They'll find out there's no poison in the cake and then they'll drop the charges."

"I hope so."

"I know so." Andy turned and headed for the bakery.

Max stood on the sidewalk lost in her own thoughts. Even if he were having an affair, she knew he couldn't murder anyone. But why did he want her to stop investigating? Was he worried about her, or was he afraid she was going to find out something?

When Max went back inside the shop, she sat down on the sofa in the showroom. She felt spent. She confided in Keiko that Andy had told her to butt out.

"But Stacy doesn't want you to butt out," Keiko said.

"No, she even told me she thinks Jennifer got her bottled water at the gym, maybe from her trainer. David West, Susan's fiancé was her trainer and his gym carried London water."

Keiko jumped up. "I'll see what I can find out about him online." She turned to go to the office and then turned back. "Unless there's something else you need me to do."

"No, I just want to sit here and think for a while."

Andy didn't want to talk about the text messages, that much was clear. Was that because he really was having an affair with Jennifer? He was keeping secrets from her; she was sure of it. What if Andy wasn't the person she thought he was? Was that possible? She didn't want to think so. She wanted things to be like they used to, when she and Andy were friends and people didn't get murdered in Crystal Shores.

Max went back to work on her alteration work, but it didn't distract her from her thoughts. At least with Keiko there she was able to get work done without having to watch the shop or the phones. Two hours later, she was in need of a break.

Keiko came running into the workroom while Max was eating one of her dad's chocolate chip cookies.

"Wait till you hear this!" Keiko exclaimed.

"Is it about David West?"

"It's as if he didn't even exist before he came to Crystal Shores a year ago. I mean, I could find lots of David Wests--it's an extremely common name--but I couldn't find him. Not in California."

"Maybe he lived somewhere else."

"Maybe. Maybe he lived in Manhattan and handled investment accounts, and maybe he bilked investors out of millions of dollars and went to jail for it." Keiko beamed proudly. "I think his real name is Damien

Whitefield. He went to jail for ten years. Just got out a year ago."

"Are you sure?"

Keiko left the room and returned with some papers.

"Here's a picture I got online, taken ten years ago when they convicted him." Max stared at the picture of a dark-haired young man with a narrow face and high cheekbones, but she didn't recognize him.

Keiko handed her another page. "Here's a picture of David West from the gym's website."

It was true. It could be the same guy. The man in the second picture had thinner hair, but it was the same narrow face and high cheekbones.

"Are you sure it's him?" Max asked. A convicted criminal would make a good addition to her suspect list. Although, even if he was a thief, that didn't make him a murderer.

"Yeah, I'm sure." Keiko compared the pictures again. "Pretty sure, anyway. What if Jennifer found out who he was and threatened to tell everyone."

"But wouldn't he just move somewhere else instead of killing her? It doesn't seem like much of a motive."

"I think he came here to find a rich wife," Keiko said. "And he found one."

"But he's engaged to Susan Brown. Are you saying there's another woman?" Max asked. She was getting confused.

"Nope. Just Susan. She's the rich wife."

"She's a schoolteacher." Max wanted to say "duh."

"She inherited property from her grandmother. When she died, she left her waterfront mansion to her daughter and six rental properties to Susan." Keiko handed her several pages of printouts from public records showing the properties Susan owned.

"Six rental properties don't make you rich," Max said. "Does it?"

"It does if they're in Crystal Shores. Besides the duplex where she lives, Susan owns a four-plex on Margarita worth about $4 million. The other five are worth $1-2 million. They're just cottages, most of them with back units like yours. It's the land that's worth so much. Developers tear down the cottages and build mini mansions. Her grandmother bought them in the Forties and Fifties when they probably cost ten or twenty thousand. She must make at least $10-15,000 a month from rental income. Maybe $20,000."

"That's a really nice income, but is it enough to kill for?" Max wondered out loud.

"Maybe he plans on talking her into selling them and bilking her out of the money. Then take off again and create a new identity in a new town."

"So, he found a rich wife. Maybe Jennifer found out and planned to blow it for him. Jennifer lived in New York around that time. Maybe she saw a story in the paper?" That was a long time to remember a news article.

"I don't know how Jennifer found out," Keiko said, "but I'll tell you something else. The gym where he works sells London water. I don't think you can get it anywhere else in town. I called a dozen places, and no one said they carried it."

"What do we do now? Tell the police?"

"Yeah, you should call that detective." Keiko gathered up all her papers.

"But he told me to butt out of it." Max didn't want to talk to him right now. He'd already made up his mind about who was guilty.

"This could get Andy off the hook," Keiko reasoned.

"What if he doesn't think they're the same person? Or even if he does, we can't prove that Jennifer knew about him. I think we need to make sure before we tell him. He doesn't even think the poison was in the water. I think he's just testing it to humor me."

Max plopped down on the sofa and sulked.

"What do we do?" Keiko asked.

"We need more evidence."

CHAPTER 14

"What's the plan?" Keiko asked.

"I don't have one," Max admitted.

"Well, that's a crappy plan."

"Thanks for the encouragement. Anyway, it's almost five. You can go on home. I'm done for the day."

"Thanks! I'm going to go home and veg out on the couch and go to bed early."

"Now that sounds like a plan."

Max cleaned up her workroom, putting everything back where it belonged. What should she do about David West? She should call Detective Cruz. But he'd probably chastise her for getting involved. And it was quite possible that David West and Damien Whitefield weren't the same person. And even if they were, there was no proof that he murdered Jennifer.

The door jingled and Eric called out her name.

"Hi, you," she said happily, giving him a hug.

"Are you okay?" he asked.

She wasn't sure. "Yeah, I'm fine. Just a bit over-whelmed."

"Well, I called Detective Cruz and told him about meeting with Jennifer on Monday. He was cross with me but didn't accuse me of anything."

"Good." She was relieved. Then she remembered that Eric had hired David West as his trainer. "Do you know anything about David West, like his background or where he's from?"

He thought for a moment. "No, he didn't talk much about himself. I think he's from the East Coast. Why?"

She showed Eric the picture of Damien Whitefield.

"I don't know." He stared at the picture. "It kinda looks like him. Do you think it's the same guy?"

"That's a really good question." She wished she knew the answer. "Do you think I should tell the police?"

"I think any excuse to call that hot detective is a good one."

She made a face at him.

"So, guess who called me today?" he said but didn't wait for her to answer. "Jonathan!"

"Who's Jonathan?" Max tried to remember. "Oh, your date from last night. I thought you didn't like him."

"He called to order flowers for Angela. She's the one who fixed us up. On the note card, he had me write, 'Thanks so much for introducing me to Eric.'"

"Wow. Now that's class."

"Isn't it? Then he told me he was nervous last night,

and he didn't think he made a good first impression, but he hoped we could go out again."

"So, what did you say?"

"I said yes, of course!"

Max laughed. "You're such a pushover. If he's as nice as he sounds, I'm glad you're giving him another chance."

"Well, I'd better get back to Daphne." With another hug he left, and Max went back to the workroom.

She'd just gotten back to work on her alterations when the door jingled again. Max sighed and went out front.

Her heart stopped. There stood David West, or whatever his name was, locking her front door. This was the worst day ever.

She managed to say, "May I help you?"

"I'm David West," he told her.

Her throat felt dry, but she managed to croak out, "Yes, I know." Maybe she should run for the back door. Could she make it in time?

"Have we met?" he asked.

"Um, I saw your picture on the website. For your gym. Jennifer got such good results I thought I might try a personal trainer. It's your fault I had to take the sleeves off her dress. She said her arms looked amazing."

"She seemed to be happy with the results we were getting."

She waited for him to tell her what he wanted. "So, what can I do for you?" she finally stammered. She took a deep calming breath like she learned in the one yoga class she had taken.

"I heard you were investigating Jennifer's murder." He came right to the point.

"What? Me? No, certainly not," she lied.

"The police have the wrong man," he told her.

"They do? I mean, of course they do. Why do you say they do? Do you know something?"

"I've met Andy. I go to his bakery every morning. They have excellent coffee," he explained. "I get their croissants sometimes. Have you ever had them?"

"Yes, they're delicious." Why were they talking about croissants right now?

"They're so light and flaky. Anyway, I'm a very good judge of character, and I just don't believe Andy did it."

"Oh. No, I'm sure he didn't." Max waited nervously to find out the real reason he came to visit her.

David seemed like he wanted to say something. Was he going to confess to her? What then? Would he kill her too? She felt panic start to take over her body.

"I have a secret," he began.

"Don't kill me!" Max cried out.

"What?" He looked at her like she was crazy. "I'm not going to kill you."

"Then why are you here?" she asked.

"I have a secret you may uncover if you haven't already. I know you've been investigating the murder, and it wouldn't take a genius to find out that my real name isn't David West."

"Uh-huh."

"You don't seem surprised." He narrowed his eyes, almost squinting at her.

"Well, lots of people change their names, you know. I mean we're not far from Hollywood. No one in Hollywood goes by their real name. Did you know Cary Grant's real name was Archibald Leach?"

"Do you always ramble like this?" he asked. "How do you ever get anything done?"

"I just ramble when I'm nervous. I seem to be nervous a lot lately." Max thought she had very good reason to be nervous at this particular moment.

"Let me just get this out," he began. "I was involved with swindling a lot of people more than twelve years ago. I was just doing what my boss told me to, though I knew it was wrong. I went to jail for almost ten years. I paid my debt to society. I came to Crystal Shores to start over."

"Uh-huh," was all Max could say.

"Again, you don't seem surprised."

"All right. I knew," she admitted. "You came here looking for a rich wife and you found Susan. Then Jennifer found out about your past and threatened to tell Susan, so you killed her." Why did she say that? She needed to stop talking, but she couldn't help herself.

"What? No! I didn't kill anyone."

"But once Susan finds out, she'll dump you for sure." Max tried to think how to keep him from killing her, but so far, she hadn't come up with any ideas. She just figured she'd keep talking. "And once Susan dumps you, you'll have to go looking for another rich wife."

"What are you talking about? Eric made you sound like someone sensible. You sound a little crazy to me."

"Are you going to tell me you didn't know Susan was rich?" she asked.

"Susan's not rich," he scoffed. "She's a schoolteacher. She drives a four-year-old Toyota Camry. She lives in a duplex. She shops at Target."

"Hey, I love Target. But all that doesn't prove anything. I'm telling you, she's rich."

"And I'm telling you, she's not."

"Is."

"Is not. What are we, ten?" He sighed. "Anyway, the reason I came here was to ask you to wait before you tell anyone. I'm having dinner with Susan tonight. I'm going to tell her everything. I should have told her long ago. Then I'm going to do the right thing and leave town."

"You are? You're not going to kill me?" This was the best day ever.

"No. I'm not a murderer! How many times do I have to tell you? I made a mistake in the past. I did my time, but it doesn't mean I'm done being punished. Losing Susan will be the hardest part of all. But I never deserved her. I just thought I could be happy again. I should have known better."

"You love her," Max said quietly.

"More than I can tell you," he admitted.

She had a thought. "But the water bottle. Jennifer got the water from you."

"The overpriced London water we sell?" He shook his head. "Jennifer never got it from us."

180

"But no one else sells it. And you're her personal trainer." She was ecstatic that he wasn't going to kill her, but she was disappointed about eliminating such a good suspect.

"We're the only place that sells it because no one else will carry it," he told her. "Jennifer talked the owner into carrying it."

"Why would she do that?" she asked.

"Because Chad works for the distributor. She got him the job, but he wasn't doing a good job of getting anyone to carry their products. She got all the water she could drink from Chad."

"So, you didn't kill her." She figured she'd just confirm it for herself.

"I've been trying to tell you that."

Max thought he seemed like a nice guy, considering. Susan would be heartbroken. "I guess I just have to figure out how to prove Chad murdered Jennifer."

She noticed David was looking at her hopefully.

"Okay, I'll let you tell her yourself. As long as you don't wait too long. She's going to take it hard. She's head over heels in love with you."

"Thank you!" He grabbed her in a hug, and she awkwardly patted him on the back.

After she let David out, she locked the door again. She decided she wouldn't stay in the shop alone without the door locked from now on. She sat down and waited for her heart rate to return to normal. She had wanted David to be the murderer. It made everything much simpler. Although, it would have been hard on Susan. Poor Susan. Should she go ahead and cancel the dress order or wait to hear from Susan? It was too late today anyway.

An evening on the sofa sounded good. Or a hot bath. But she wouldn't find out who the killer was on the sofa or in the bath. Although it might be safer. She spent a good ten minutes deciding if she should play it safe or not. She put the pepper spray in her pocket and locked up the shop.

Just after six, she walked through the door of the Crazy Fox. She sat at the bar and asked Burt for a Ketel One on the rocks. After all, she deserved a stiff drink after the day she'd had. She waved hello to two regulars, Frank and Ernie, who were at the other end of the bar watching the football game.

"How's the murder investigation going?" Burt asked, handing her the drink.

"Shh! Does everyone know I'm trying to find the murderer?" she whispered.

"Just the people in Crystal Shores. I'm pretty sure the people in Laguna Beach have no idea." He laughed at his own joke.

"Very funny. I have a few suspects. I have no idea if any of them did it. It's hard to believe people are capable of murder. Maybe evil people you've never met, but not someone you've actually know."

"Who are your suspects?" he asked.

"I don't think I should tell you." She knew he was friends with Chad. Or at least he saw a lot of him since Chad played in the band four nights a week.

"Max, it sounds like you could use some help. I am a

good listener, which means I've heard a lot. I might know something that would help."

Max took a sip of her vodka and thought it over. "Chad."

"Didn't do it." Burt reached for a glass and rinsed it off in a sink of soapy water. "He just doesn't have it in him."

"Yeah, you're probably right." She'd known Burt for years, but she didn't know how close he was with Chad. What if Burt told Chad that she suspected him? What if he wrote the note? She rattled the ice cubes around in her drink with her straw. "I'd still like to talk to him. He's playing tonight, right?"

"The band's not playing tonight. They said Chad couldn't make it and they couldn't find a replacement on such short notice."

"Darn. I really wanted to talk with him." She had hoped to talk to him in a nice, crowded bar. "I wonder if he's still at Jennifer's house."

"I heard he was staying somewhere else. Her mom kicked him out."

"Ouch. That's harsh." Max paused. "Wait. Does she have the right to do that? I thought he was supposed to inherit everything."

"We'll have to wait and see, I guess. Her mom's next of kin, so I guess she's in control for the short term."

She waited while Burt refilled drinks for Frank and Ernie.

"Where's Chad staying?" she asked when he got back.

Burt seemed uncomfortable. "On a boat," he said.

"Whose boat, Burt?" Max was pretty sure she already knew the answer.

"Adam's."

Adam Gold owned the Carriage House restaurant, along with a house on Zinnia Street and a yacht. The yacht rarely left the harbor but was most often used to entertain people, usually 20-something women. Max knew it well since she had dated Adam for six months until she caught him making out with another woman behind the restaurant after closing. She hadn't gone on a date since.

"Well, I guess if I want to talk to Chad, I'll have to go to the boat." That seemed like a really bad idea. If he were the killer, then pepper spray wasn't likely to protect her. Who could she get to go with her?

"So, who else you got for suspects?" Burt asked Max to change the subject.

Max wasn't sure if she should mention Nancy. She wouldn't want word to get back to Nancy or Richard that she was asking questions about her. "I was wondering about Chad's sister Kelly. Do you know anything about her?"

"Chad's sister lives in San Francisco. I don't think she's been in town for a month. She usually comes and watches him play when she visits."

"Okay, so that's a bust. Do you know any of the people she worked with at the real estate office?" she asked, hoping she was being subtle.

"I've met Nancy. There was no love lost there. She doesn't come here regularly, but Frank," Burt motioned to the end of the bar, "used to work with Nancy."

"Thanks, Burt. You were right. You did help," she told him, and then went over to the two men.

"Max, sit down and join us," Frank said. "We're just watching the game."

"Nice to see you Max," Ernie said. "How's Richard?"

"He's great," Max answered.

After what she thought was an acceptable amount of small talk, she got to the point.

"Frank, Burt tells me you know Nancy Addison."

"I used to work with her." He kept glancing over her shoulder at the TV screen while he talked to her. "She knows her stuff. I tried to get her to come back and work with me again, but she said she's happy where she is."

"I heard Jennifer Burns stole away some of her clients. Is that true?" she asked.

He laughed, which seemed strange to her. "She did. And Nancy stole them right back. Plus, a couple of extras for good measure."

She heard a man ask Burt where he could find Chad. Not him again. She turned around in her seat away from the voice hoping to be unnoticed. Apparently, she was not successful.

"Max?"

"Detective Cruz," she said, turning around as if she just realized he was there. "What brings you here tonight?"

"I was going to ask you the same question," he said.

"Just visiting some friends," she told him. "I have many friends in this town."

"You certainly do," he admitted. "The bartender tells me you are planning to go see Chad."

"I am, actually. I was thinking of stopping by to say hi and see how he's doing." She was angry at Burt for a moment, and then she thought it would be much better to question him with Detective Cruz there to protect her. She'd already had one scare today, and that was enough.

"I'd rather you didn't," he said.

"I see." Max took a sip of her drink. "Well, I'll keep that in mind."

"I'm worried about you, Max."

She turned back around and faced him. For a moment it sounded like he actually cared about her. Of course, he was just doing his job, keeping citizens safe. "So go with me. You know if you don't, I'm going to go there alone. Which could be dangerous. This way you get to keep me safe."

"Nope. Not happening."

Detective Cruz didn't think it was safe for her to go see Chad alone. Did that mean he still considered Chad a suspect? That would mean he wasn't completely convinced Andy was guilty.

They sat there not speaking. Max sipped her water and waited.

"Fine," he said, obviously exasperated. "Let's go." They stepped outside into the cool night. "Where's your car?" he asked.

"I don't have one," she admitted.

"No car? I think you're the first person I've met since I moved here who doesn't have a car. Fine, we'll take mine." His patrol car was parked on the street. He opened the door and she got in.

They drove north on Coast Highway in silence. Max told him to make a left on 17th, and Detective Cruz told her he knew the way. He sounded grumpy. A few minutes later, they turned into the marina parking lot. The bright lights shone on a dozen or so luxury cars. They got out of the car, and Max led him to the gate. She punched in the code, hoping it hadn't changed.

She walked down the wharf with the detective following her. They passed several multi-million-dollar yachts until they came to a forty-foot boat, modest by local standards. They climbed aboard and went over to the sliding glass door.

Detective Cruz rapped his knuckles on the glass. After a few minutes, Chad appeared and slid the door open. He stared at them and finally spoke, sounding confused.

"Detective, what are you doing here? Max?"

"I just wanted to talk with you, if you have a few moments," Max said. "May we come in?"

"Sure." He stepped back to let them into the small cabin. The interior appeared just the way Max remembered. It was small but comfortable. Clothes were tossed on a brown leather sofa, and dishes sat in the sink. "I heard you arrested Andy. Are you sure you have the right guy? He sure didn't seem like the type." He picked up the clothes off the sofa and invited them to sit down. He grabbed a chair from the dinette set and sat down across from them.

"Detective Cruz thinks Andy and Jennifer were having an affair," Max said.

"What? No way. He's not her type."

"I'm sorry to tell you this, but it's true. We have numerous texts back and forth between them," Cruz told him. "They were keeping a secret."

"Is that it?" Max jumped in. "Is that all you have? They had a secret? It could be anything. It doesn't mean they were having an affair."

"I agree with Max," Chad said.

"We have the right guy in custody," Cruz said. "I'm just trying to keep Max out of trouble."

"How do you know he didn't do it?" Max said, pointing to Chad. "Sorry," she added.

"It's okay," Chad said. "I'd be asking the same question if I were you."

"What's the motive?" the detective asked.

"Money!" How obvious could it be? "Jennifer changed her will, making him her sole beneficiary."

The two men looked at each other. "Should you tell her, or should I?" Chad asked.

"Go right ahead."

"The will said I became the sole beneficiary as soon as we got married. She was worth a whole lot more to me alive than dead. At least until after the wedding. Now, all I have is my car. I suppose I'll have to sell it. I can't even afford the insurance."

"Darn. You were my best suspect." Max sat back in her chair and scowled. "Well, I'm out of suspects," she admitted.

"I have another one for you, Max," Chad said. "Her

mother. That's who's going to inherit everything. Once we got married, she would have gotten nothing."

"Her mother hadn't seen her for months," Detective Cruz said.

"That's what she said..." Max said.

"How do you know what she said?" Detective Cruz interrupted Max. "Were you questioning her? I told you to stay out of it."

"I went with Fiona to pay our respects. Remember? I told you. Sonia just happened to mention that she hadn't talked to her daughter for six months. But the truth is, Jennifer saw her mother at the Cheshire Cat the night she was murdered."

"And how do you know that?" the detective asked Max.

"Because my friend Olivia had drinks with Jennifer the night she died. Sonia sat next to her at the bar. She could have slipped the Cyanide into her drink."

"That seems a little far-fetched, don't you think?" Cruz asked.

"Not really," Chad joined in. "She certainly had a motive. She was being written out of the will."

"If she was going to kill someone, why not kill you?" Max asked. "Why kill her own child?"

"Jennifer isn't her own child," Chad explained. "She was her stepdaughter. She adopted her when she was four years old. From what Jennifer told me, Sonia was always jealous of her."

"I kind of feel sorry for Jennifer, being raised by Sonia," Max said. "No wonder she was..." Max realized she shouldn't complete the sentence with Chad in the same room.

"You can say it. She was high maintenance, to say the least. But I did love her. You just didn't know her the way I did."

At least someone loved Jennifer and was grieving her loss. Max felt kind of sorry for Jennifer, even though she was gone.

"Now I suppose you're going to want to talk to Mrs. Burns. Come on, Max. I'll give you a ride home."

"Would you like to come with me to question Sonia?"

"Not a chance. I'll go see her tomorrow and ask her why she lied to us. I want you to stay away from her."

Max reluctantly agreed. She was too tired to argue, anyway.

Max climbed the steps up to her apartment. Time for some stew, finally. She put some in a bowl and microwaved it. She sat at her kitchen table not tasting her dinner, wondering if Detective Cruz had questioned Sonia. Then she realized the stew wasn't very good. How could she screw up something so simple?

There wasn't a lot of evidence to charge Sonia with murder. None as far as she knew. Maybe the detective was such a good interrogator that Sonia would confess. Then, Andy would be off the hook. She wondered what took them so long to test the cake. Once they found out there was no poison in it, there'd surely drop the charges. Wouldn't they?

She suddenly felt lonely, sitting in her kitchen with a half-eaten bowl of stew. She wished her mom were there for her to talk to. She could always make sense of things, and nothing made sense to Max right now. Maybe she should check with her dad and see what he was doing. No, she was going to have to get used to being alone. After all, there was no dad in New York. And no Olivia or Eric or Keiko. But she had some friends in New York. Not friends like she had here, but she'd get to know them better and she'd make new friends too. Go on some dates. In such a big city she was bound to find someone to fall in love with.

She cleaned out her bowl and put it away. It was only 8:30. Five minutes later, she sat on her dad's sofa picking out a movie while he made popcorn. Why not take advantage of having him nearby while she could? Besides, he made the best buttered popcorn.

CHAPTER 15

*M*ax sat at her dad's kitchen table the next morning staring at her bowl of oatmeal. She pulled the red stone out of her pocket, where she put it every morning since she had found it, just in case it was good luck. She rubbed the smooth surface absentmindedly.

"Earth to Max," Richard said, sitting across from her.

"Oh, sorry." Her father looked worried, and she hated to be the cause of it. She decided to tell him what was on her mind anyway. "I was just wondering if Sonia could really kill her own daughter. I mean, even if she wasn't her biological child, she still raised her."

"It's hard to believe anyone we know is capable of murder. But she had a motive and you found out she was with her not long before Jennifer died."

"Yeah. She had opportunity. And she lied about it. At least it's another suspect. I wish the tests would come back on the cake samples. That would totally clear Andy."

"If there's no poison in it," her dad said, getting up to get himself another cup of coffee.

"What? Dad, there's no way there's poison in it."

"Of course, you're right. I don't know why I said that. More coffee?" he asked.

Max shook her head. "I'll be happy when this is all over," she admitted. "I'm glad I'm not a real detective."

"You don't fool me, Max. You can't stop thinking about it, no matter how many times I told you to stay out of it."

"Sorry, Dad. Yes, you, Andy and Detective Cruz all told me the same thing. But I just had to do something. Besides, I know everyone better than Detective Cruz, so sometimes I see things he doesn't." Max still hadn't told her father about the note. She didn't want to worry him.

"You're being careful, right?" She heard the worry in his voice. "If the murderer thinks you're onto him, it could be dangerous."

"I'm being careful," she reassured him.

"Maybe Sonia has confessed by now, and we can all go back to our normal lives."

"I hope so. Well, I'd better get ready for work." She got up and put her bowl in the dishwasher. "Dad, do you think I dress like a banker?"

"A very stylish banker. Why do you ask?"

"Keiko thinks I should kick it up a notch. I suggested she tone it down when Darlene gets back, and she said I need to tone it up."

"Do you want the truth, Max?" he asked.

"Of course." As long as the truth was what she wanted to hear. "I wouldn't have asked otherwise."

"Well," her dad said, pausing as if to find the right words, "you dress like you're forty or fifty. Your wardrobe would be perfect for a librarian."

"It would?" She hoped he meant a very stylish librarian.

"I agree with Keiko. You are a creative, interesting young woman. You should dress like it."

"Okay. I'll have to see what's in my closet." Black slacks, sweaters, and boring blouses. That's what was in her closet. When had she become so dull?

"Didn't your mom bring you back something when we came back from Nepal?"

"She always brought me back something." Her mother loved to drag her dad off to faraway, exotic places, although Richard would have been content staying at home. She always brought back presents for Max.

"Did you ever wear them?"

"Sure," Max whined. "Once or twice. Did she think I was boring too?"

"Nobody thinks you're boring. You just dress like you are."

Max went up the stairs to her apartment. She hardly ever threw anything away, so she was pretty sure the skirt from Nepal still hung in the back of her closet somewhere. She found it and pulled it out. She smiled when she saw the paisley print with a myriad of different colors: reds, purples, blues, and greens. What did she have that would go with it? She went through her blouses and found a lilac long sleeve t-shirt that matched one of the colors. She put it on, but it still needed something, so she went through a pile of belts and other accessories she had in a box. She dug out a red sash and wrapped it around her waist. She put on ballet flats and checked herself out in the mirror. I look ridiculous, she thought. Or do I? I look like someone else. Like a designer? Maybe.

She resisted the urge to change her clothes since she would be late if she took any more time getting ready. She grabbed her purse and headed down the street to the shop.

When she arrived, Keiko was already waiting outside. Keiko clapped her hands.

"I love your outfit!" she said.

"Really?" Max unlocked the door, and they went inside.

"Yes, really. And look. We're coordinated. My dress matches your sash."

Keiko wore a red baby doll dress with lace trim and had a large red bow on top of her head.

"We're quite the pair," Max agreed.

The door jingled and Curtis came through the door.

"What have you got for me today?" Max asked.

"Wow, check you out. You look great! Both of you. I don't actually have a package today," he admitted. "I brought something for Keiko."

"For me?" Keiko asked.

He reached into his pocket and unwrapped some

paper. There were two small toy creatures, less than two inches tall. He held them out to her.

"They're *Summiko Gurashi*," he said.

"Things in the corner," Keiko muttered.

"Right! They had them at the stationery store, and they just made me think of you."

"Because they're shy and hide in the corner?" she asked, scowling.

"No," he laughed. "Because they're *kawaii*."

She took the little cat and penguin.

"They are very *kawaii*," she said.

"So, you like them?"

"I like them very much. Thank you."

"I'm glad. Well, I'll see you next time a package arrives. I hope it's soon!"

After he left, Keiko stood staring at the little animals in her hands. She shrugged and turned to Max.

"Where were we?" she asked.

"Why don't you check on the appointments for tomorrow and call them and confirm."

"Okay," Keiko said and retreated to the office.

The door jingled, and a handsome older man stuck his head in.

"Excuse me?" he said. "The yarn store next door seems to be closed. I was supposed to meet a lady named Teresa about my cat."

"Oh, are you the owner?"

"Yes. I'm Simon Abbot." He shook Max's hand. "She told me to stop by anytime, but I guess they don't open until later."

"They open at noon. I'll give her a call. Have a seat. Make yourself comfortable."

Max made the call but got Teresa's voice mail. While she was leaving a message, Simon seemed anything but comfortable sitting in the overstuffed chair surrounded by bridal gowns and accessories.

"Maybe just have her call me," he said and wrote down his number for her.

Just then, Teresa walked in holding Josie in her arms. The cat looked completely content and not at all interested in its real owner.

"There you are, Cat," Simon said. "What are you doing wandering off? You've never done that before." He held out his hand to Teresa. "I'm Simon Abbott."

"I'm Teresa," she told him and reached out her hand to him.

He held her hand for several seconds. "It's very nice to meet you. Thank you for going to the trouble to post signs around the neighborhood. I was quite worried."

"It was no trouble. Honestly, I hoped no one would claim her." Then she said to the cat, "I'm going to miss you, Josie."

"Josie? Who's Josie?" Simon asked.

"Oh, sorry. That's what I've been calling her," Teresa explained. "What's her name?"

"Actually, she doesn't have one. I just call her Cat. My wife was supposed to name her. When she came home from the hospital."

"Oh," Teresa said, sounding disappointed. "Will she be coming home soon?"

"No, actually, she passed away."

"I'm so sorry!" Teresa reached out and patted Simon on his arm.

"She always wanted a cat, but I always said no. I didn't want cat hair getting on everything. The last time she went in the hospital, I decided to surprise her, and I got the cat. She passed away a year ago yesterday. It's funny, but she told me I could be sad for a year, but then I needed to get on with living. She was very practical that way."

"I'm sure she just wanted you to be happy," Teresa said.

"I know," he agreed. "I just don't know if I'm done being sad yet."

Max watched the two seniors and couldn't help but think they made a perfect couple. They talked for a while, then Simon took the cat, who looked a bit put out about leaving Teresa's arms. He thanked them both and left.

"I bet he calls you," Max told her.

Teresa giggled.

"He was cute, it's true. But I don't know if he's over his wife yet."

"That doesn't mean you can't hang out. You know, go out for coffee or lunch or something."

"I would like that," she admitted.

"Have you ever been married, Teresa?" Max asked. "If you don't mind me asking."

"Not at all. I was engaged once to a boy I grew up with." Teresa got a faraway look in her eyes. "We always kind of knew we were going to be together. We got engaged before he went off to college."

"Did the long-distance thing not work?" Max's first real boyfriend went off to college miles away. It lasted less than three months after he left.

"No, it worked fine. We wrote letters every week for the first year. I still have them," she said wistfully. "Then, he had a summer job at the sawmill. He was killed in an accident at the mill."

"Oh, I'm so sorry!" Max said.

"It was fifty years ago, Max. I should be over it by now!"

"Maybe you should be. But you're not, are you?"

"No, I suppose not. I never met anyone else I felt the same way about. I always regretted not having a family. But I have Fiona, and my nephews and all the grand-nieces and nephews."

"But maybe it's not too late to feel that way again."

"At my age?" She laughed. "I was lucky enough to find the love of my life once. I'm happy I had him while I did. Lightning doesn't strike twice, you know."

Maybe not, Max thought. But maybe sometimes it does.

CHAPTER 16

"*O*kay, I've called everyone," Keiko announced, coming out of the office. "You've got three appointments for tomorrow, and they're all confirmed. Is it usually that busy on Saturdays?"

"Busier when Darlene's here." Max dusted the glass shelf that held the tiaras. "There'll be some drop ins too, probably. There always are." Saturdays could be crazy.

"I went ahead and confirmed for Monday too. Here, let me do that." Keiko took the feather duster from Max.

"Great. I didn't even have a chance to double check my schedule for today. Tell me there aren't any appointments I've forgotten about." Max walked over to the row of gowns and started fluffing the skirts absentmindedly.

"There are no appointments. But you did tell Tiffany you'd get back to her with the estimate for her dress."

200

"That's right. The least favorite part of my job, next to taking out stitches. Well, I'd better get to work. I'll be in the office if you need me. I hate spreadsheets."

"I'm quite good with numbers and spreadsheets. Can I help?"

"Seriously? Come on, let's get to work."

Keiko redesigned the spreadsheet Max used for her estimates, making it much easier to use. It was almost twelve by the time they had Tiffany's estimate completed.

"What should we do for lunch?" Max asked, standing up from the desk and stretching her arms.

"I brought lunch," Keiko said.

"Oh. Then what do I want to do for lunch?" she asked herself.

"I brought lunch for both of us." She got up and pulled two plastic containers out of the office refrigerator. She handed one to Max, along with a fork and napkin. They went into the workroom, and Max covered the worktable with brown paper she used for pattern making and impromptu tablecloths. She opened her container, and there were two eyes staring back at her.

"It's a bear," Max said.

"Yes." Keiko grinned. "Made out of rice and soy sauce. The eyes and mouth are seaweed. There's also some chicken and fruit on the side."

"It's adorable." Max stared at the creature. "I don't know if I want to eat it. It's too cute."

"It's for eating, not saving."

"If you say so." Max took out her phone and took a

picture. "Okay, now I can eat it. Did you make it yourself?"

"Yes. My mother only knows how to make bologna sandwiches."

"Where did you learn to do it?" Max asked.

"On the internet. You can learn how to do anything on the Internet."

"Cool," Max said, approvingly.

Keiko offered her chopsticks, but Max decided to use a fork. If she used chopsticks, they'd be there all day. They'd just finished eating when they heard a knock on the back door. Max got up and unlocked it and let Andy in.

"Hi," he said. Was she imagining that he seemed cooler to her?

"We're just finishing lunch. What's up?"

"Does something have to be up?"

"No, of course not. Sit down. Would you like some tea? We just made a pot."

"What was for lunch?"

"A bear," Max answered.

"A bear?"

"Seriously. I'll show you," she said and showed him the picture. "Keiko made it."

"I'll clean this up," Keiko said, picking up the containers. "You guys can talk."

Max poured Andy a cup of tea.

"So, how's the investigation going?" Andy asked.

"I knew something was up," Max said. "Well, right now, Sonia is my prime suspect."

"Sonia? Jennifer's mom?"

"Yeah, it turns out she was going to be cut out of the will as soon as Jennifer married Chad. Plus, she saw Jennifer the night she died and lied about it."

"Boy, that's creepy." He made a sour face. "Do you think she did it?"

"I'm not sure. But I think you'd be off the hook if you could prove you weren't having an affair with Jennifer."

"I didn't realize they were basing so much of their case on our texts. I just explained to Detective Cruz why we were calling and texting so much. And what the secret was I was keeping from Stacy."

"What was the secret?"

"I'm going to tell Stacy tonight, so I guess I can tell you. I'm buying her a house."

"A house? This was all about a house?"

"Stacy fell in love with a cottage on Zinnia. It just went on the market last Friday, and I got in touch with Jennifer right away to see if I could buy it for her. For us. I wanted to make sure everything was going to work out before I told her. I told Stacy we couldn't afford it."

"Can you? Afford it, I mean?"

"My parents are helping. They're happy to have me back home, and they love Stacy. I wanted to do it on my own, but I haven't saved up nearly enough for a down payment. And I knew how much Stacy loved that house."

"So that's the secret," Max said. "You big dummy. You should have told everyone sooner."

"Yeah, I didn't realize they were making such a big

deal out of all the texts. They were completely innocent, but I guess I can see how they could be taken the
wrong way. So can you keep a secret for a few hours?"

"No problem."

"Thanks," Andy said, leaving out the back door. "But
just to be safe, I think I'll keep Stacy away from you."

Since Friday afternoons were usually quiet, Max
liked to go over next week's schedule. Darlene would
be back, so Max planned to take Keiko with her to her
favorite fabric store in downtown L.A.

"For Tiffany's dress, I think the fabric should be
light, but not flimsy, so I think..." Max stopped mid-
sentence.

"Did you see something?" Keiko asked and turned
around to follow Max's gaze.

"It was Josie. She walked right by." Max got up and
opened the front door in time to see the cat walk into
the Knitpickers next door.

"Josie sure likes yarn," Keiko said.

"Or Teresa," Max added. She went back to talking
about the fabric for Tiffany's dress. She looked up
when the door jingled.

Susan Brown entered and greeted them both. Max
couldn't tell what her mood was, but she seemed serious. Keiko made an excuse and went in the office.

"Have a seat," Max said, and they both sat down.
Susan didn't seem like she knew where to start.

"Are you here to cancel the dress?" Max asked.

"Actually, no," Susan said and saw the look on Max's
face. "You look surprised, and I don't blame you. David

told me he came and talked to you. I'm glad you know the whole story."

"So, you're still going to marry him?"

"We had a long talk. In fact, we had several long talks. He's basically a good guy. He just got caught up in something and didn't know how to get out of it."

"I have to admit, I really think he loves you," Max said.

"I believe he does. I'm actually more convinced than ever."

"Then I'm happy for you." Susan didn't quite have the same glow she had the last time she saw her, but that glow had to wear off eventually. Love had hurdles, and they had weathered their first one. It was a big one, that was for sure.

"Thank you," Susan said. "Of course, there will be a prenup," she added. "He actually insisted on it."

"Good," Max said. "I'm glad to hear it. Well, your dress is ordered, and I'll be calling you in a couple of months for your first fitting."

Susan stood up and gave her a big hug. "Thank you for not judging me."

"You love each other," Max said smiling. "I don't know a lot about love, but I know it when I see it. I think you two kids have a chance."

Susan laughed happily and gave Max another hug.

After Susan left, Teresa stopped by. "Josie's back," she announced.

"I know," Max said. "We saw her."

"I don't know how to get in touch with Simon. Can

you see if you can find his number? I'd rather not have to put flyers up all over the neighborhood again."

"No need. He gave me his number when he was here before. I'll get it for you."

"Thanks. Isn't it funny she came back?" Teresa asked.

"We don't think it's funny at all," Keiko said. "We think she likes you."

"Maybe she doesn't like living with a man who calls her Cat," Max added.

"I think you're being hard on him. He thinks of Josie as his wife's cat, and I think he's not ready to let go of her memory. It's like he's still waiting for her to come home and give the cat a name."

"Well, here's his number. Give him a call."

"Thanks," Teresa said and went back to her shop.

Max knew the one thing she should be working on was the alterations for Sylvia Stone's gown. If she didn't get it done today, she'd have to work on Sunday to finish it. She told Keiko to watch the shop while she got to work. She heard the door jingle and hoped it was something Keiko could handle. Suddenly, Sonia appeared in the workroom door. Her hair appeared uncombed, and her beige tracksuit looked like she'd slept in it.

"What are you going around telling the police about me?" she demanded.

"What are you talking about?" Of course, she had a pretty good idea.

Sonia crossed her arms and glared at Max. "You told them I saw Jennifer the night she died."

"Well, you did, didn't you?"

"That's not the point!" Sonia's face got redder.

"Then what is the point?" Max asked.

"I didn't kill her!" she shouted.

"I never said you did." Max wondered if Keiko was calling the police. She hoped so. "But why did you lie about seeing her that night. You told us you hadn't seen her for six months. You told the police the same thing."

"I knew they'd find out about the will, and I'd be a suspect. You don't have to try hard to find out we didn't get along. Hell, she didn't get along with much of anybody."

"So, you knew you would inherit everything if she died before she married Chad."

"Yeah, I knew," Sonia admitted. "I don't know if he knew, though."

"Chad? He knew."

"Then who the hell killed her?" She grabbed Max's arm. "Why haven't you figured it out yet?"

"I wish I knew, Sonia," Max told her, removing Sonia's hand from her arm and trying to stay calm.

"You just better stop spreading lies about me," Sonia said and stormed out.

Keiko stuck her head in. "Are you okay? I was about to call 911."

"Yeah, I'm fine. I've had about enough of people coming in here to tell me they didn't kill Jennifer. It's unnerving." She walked to the front door and locked it. "Everyone's going to have to knock from now on."

"I didn't kill Jennifer too." Keiko smiled. "I just thought I'd get it out of the way so you can get some work done. Maybe I'll start a list, and everyone can just sign their name if they didn't kill her."

"That's a great idea," Max said. "It will make solving the murder much easier. We can just see who's not on the list, and that's our murderer!"

Keiko laughed. "It seems to be the best plan we have come up with so far!"

"If only it were that easy," Max sighed and went back to her sewing. A little while later, she heard a knock at the door. Keiko came back to tell her she had another visitor: Simon Abbot.

"I hope I'm not disturbing you," he said.

"Not at all. Did you come to get your cat? Is the yarn store closed?" Max asked.

"No, they're open. I just wanted to speak with you before I went to pick up Josie."

Max smiled at Simon using Teresa's name for his cat. "Sure. What can I do for you?"

He glanced around the room and seemed to be unsure of what to say. "I just wanted to ask your advice, if you don't mind. I mean, if it's not too much of an imposition."

"Of course, I don't mind." Max's curiosity was piqued. "What is it?"

"I was wondering if Teresa was single."

"Oh!" Max understood the reason for the visit. She figured she might as well give him a nudge in the right direction. "Yes, she's single and unattached. I think if you asked her to coffee or lunch, she'd be happy to join you."

He grinned. "That's just wonderful. I think I'll do that." He shook Max's hand. "I'd better go get Josie."

Max went back to the workroom to work on the alterations. She was deep in thought when there was another knock on the door. She heard Keiko greet Teresa, and she was about to get up when Teresa stepped into the workroom. "He asked me out!" she told Max, beaming.

"That's wonderful, Teresa." At least someone had a love life. "He seems like a very nice man."

"And handsome," Teresa said. "We're going to lunch on Sunday."

"That's wonderful. What about Josie?" Max asked. "She seems to like hanging out at the yarn shop. How's he going to keep her from coming to visit you?"

"That's the best part!" Teresa seemed positively giddy. "He's going to drop her off every day and she can spend the day with Fiona and me. She'll be our shop cat. Then when we close, we'll drop her off at his place."

"It sounds like the perfect arrangement."

"I'll get to see him almost every day. We had such a nice talk. We have so many things in common." She frowned slightly. "If this works out, it will be hard going back home to Canada next month. We'll see how the long-distance thing works this time."

"Just take one day at a time, Teresa," Max told her. "And enjoy it!"

"Thank you, Max, I will." Teresa floated out of the room.

While Max sewed, she thought about the secret she was keeping from Keiko. What if she heard it from someone else? She finished with the alterations a little before six. She wouldn't have to work on Sunday after all. She emerged from the workroom to find Keiko running the vacuum cleaner. It was about time she told her about the job.

"I need to tell you something," Max started.

"You seem very serious. Should I sit down?" Keiko asked

"No, I mean, if you want. Sure, let's sit down." Max sat down and Keiko sat across from her. "I was offered a position as an assistant designer with Bissette, the design firm I used to work for."

Keiko blinked and stared at her blankly. "You're leaving?"

"I've always planned to move back to New York," she explained. "It's a great opportunity."

Keiko said nothing. She just sat there, unsmiling. Then she spoke. "Do not expect me to be happy about it. You must make your own decisions, but I would prefer you stay here."

"I want to be a designer," Max told her.

"I told you before. You are a designer. If you are unable to see that, then perhaps you need to go to New York to learn what I already know." Keiko blinked back tears.

"I'm sorry you're upset." Max hadn't expected this reaction.

"What about Tiffany's dress? We were going to

make it together." Keiko walked into the office and got her bag. "I'm going home. I'll see you tomorrow."

"Okay, Keiko. We'll talk about Tiffany's dress. I'm not leaving right away."

Keiko didn't answer her. She just walked out the front door without a goodbye.

CHAPTER 17

*M*ax sat in the showroom thinking about everything that had happened over the past few days. Now she had even more on her mind. Sonia must have been the one to murder Jennifer. But something just didn't seem right.

She went to her office and got her notebook. She went over the names she had listed under "Suspects." She added Sonia to the list.

The phone rang. Detective Cruz thought she would like to know they were dropping charges for Andy Fuller. The tests they had done on the cake samples had come in and there was no poison in the cake.

"The most dangerous thing in that cake was chocolate," he told her.

"That's wonderful! Thank you for calling me and letting me know. It's a huge relief."

"For you, maybe," he sighed. "I still have a murderer to catch."

"What about Sonia?"

"I don't know. I interviewed her, and that definitely was not a typical mother-daughter relationship. And she did have a motive. But there were so many people around at the bar it's hard to believe she could slip the cyanide into the drink undetected. Besides, from what witnesses have told me, it wasn't a planned meeting. They just happened to run into each other that night at the bar. It seems unlikely she walked around with poison in her purse just waiting to run into her daughter so she could kill her."

"So, it's back to square one."

"Yes, it sure looks like it. And now that Andy is no longer a suspect, you'll quit snooping?"

"Yep! I mean if I had been snooping, then I would quit."

"Right."

Max hung up the phone and smiled. What a relief! Her friend was off the hook, and she could quit trying to solve the murder. Which was good, because she didn't have any more ideas. Although she didn't like having a murderer walking around free, especially one that had threatened her.

No, she told herself. I'm done with this investigating. I never was any good at it anyway. What did I accomplish? All I managed to do was to find out who wasn't the killer.

Still, if there were a murderer in their midst, he might kill again. He might even kill her like he had threatened.

She read the list of suspects again. She tried to forget what she thought she knew about all of them.

She remembered what Detective Cruz had told her about Andy and Jennifer having an affair. She'd actually started to wonder if he could have had an affair, but she never thought he was a killer.

She stared at the name Stacy written on the page. It was funny to think she had a 3.7 GPA in college. She wondered if she took all easy classes to get such good grades. But she was going to school to become a nurse, and those classes couldn't all have been easy. Max had a friend who wanted to be a nurse, but she had such a hard time with chemistry class. Chemistry. You might learn about things like poison in chemistry class. No, she shook her head. We're talking about Stacy.

But what if Stacy was smarter than she seemed to be? What if she thought Andy and Jennifer were having an affair? The police had thought so. Maybe Stacy did too.

But there was no poison in the cake. Chocolate cake, she thought to herself. Something seemed wrong.

She called Detective Cruz's number and left a message. "When you said the most dangerous thing in the cake was chocolate, I just wanted to check and make sure you weren't being literal. There wasn't any chocolate cake in the box. Jennifer had decided to go with something non-chocolate. Maybe you don't even know what flavor the cake was. I mean, I'm sure you have everything under control. Oh, never mind. Just disregard this message. Sorry!"

Boy, wait till he got her message. He'd think she had a screw loose.

There was a knock on the front door. Max saw

Stacy through the glass. She unlocked the door and let Stacy in.

"Did you hear they dropped the charges?" Stacy asked with a big smile on her face.

"I just heard." She hugged Stacy. She must be crazy to think for even a moment this sweet young woman was capable of murder. "Sit down for a minute. You must be so relieved."

Max sat down. Stacy sat across from her. "Thanks so much for all your help. I'm lucky to have such good friends. Detective Cruz said you found the water bottle and they think it has cyanide in it. I think they're questioning her trainer."

"Yeah, weird how the police didn't find the bottle the night of the murder when they searched the shop."

"I guess they didn't look under the desk."

"Under the desk?" Max asked.

"Oh, yeah." Stacy's smile disappeared. "That's where he said they found it."

"And weird how she drank the water even though cyanide has a funny taste."

"What are you getting at?" Stacy asked.

"Nothing." Max stood up. She had a bad feeling in the pit of her stomach. "It's just weird. I'm so glad this is over. I knew Andy wasn't guilty. I was worried because they didn't seem to be investigating anyone else. I mean, there were plenty of people who didn't like Jennifer. There were so many suspects. That was the hardest part about trying to figure out who the murderer was – there were just so many suspects."

"You're rambling." Stacy leaned back in her chair and folded her arms.

"Am I?"

The phone rang and Max rushed over to pick it up. She was relieved to hear Detective Cruz's voice.

"I got your message. I checked with the lab to make sure. The cake in the box was chocolate. Are you sure there wasn't any chocolate cake in the box?"

"Yep, I'm sure," she answered.

"Do you think the boxes could have been switched?"

She turned around to see Stacy holding a gun on her. "Could be."

"Is everything okay?" he asked.

"Hang up the phone," Stacy hissed.

"Everything's fine," Max said. "Gotta go." She put the phone down.

"What was that all about," Stacy asked coldly.

"Just my dad inviting me over for dinner," she lied.

"Do you think I'm an idiot?" Stacy laughed. "Oh, that's right, you do. Just because I don't get sarcasm doesn't mean I'm not intelligent."

"You switched the boxes." Max stared at the gun pointing at her. How was she going to get out of this one?

The phone rang again.

"Don't answer it," Stacy ordered. It rang four times and then stopped. "I knew the cops would show up that night. I couldn't have them finding poison in the cake. Although, I knew they'd suspect Andy before they suspected me. And even though I didn't want him to go to jail, it was better him than me."

"So, you made up the story about Andy and Jennifer having an affair." Max watched Stacy as she walked over to the door and pulled down the blind.

"Oh, that part was true." Stacy sounded sure of herself. "Although I don't think she threatened to tell me. I don't think she wanted anyone to find out either."

"That's what I told Detective Cruz! I still don't believe they were having an affair."

"I saw the texts. 'Stacy can't find out.' Andy was so careless."

"That wasn't about an affair," Max told her.

"Yes, it was!" Stacy was yelling now. "I saw the texts! Stop disagreeing with me!"

"Listen to me." Max thought she'd better try to calm her down. She'd promised Andy not to tell Stacy about the house, but these were very special circumstances. "Andy told me you fell in love with a house on Zinnia Street. Do you know the one?"

"Of course. I've loved that house since I first saw it. And then it came on the market. Andy said we couldn't afford it."

"He made an offer on it."

"What are you talking about? He did not. We don't have the money."

"His parents were giving him a big down payment. As soon as it went on the market, he got in touch with Jennifer and told her he wanted to buy it. He was going to surprise you."

"Oh, that's amazing!" Stacy smiled. Max used to think it was such a sweet smile. "He is such a wonderful guy. But you knew that."

"Yeah, he's great," Max agreed. Except his taste in women was terrible.

Stacy still stood holding the gun pointed at her. "Well, this is awkward. So, he wasn't having an affair, after all."

"Nope."

"I just wish he hadn't kept it a secret from me. What was I supposed to think, with all their texting back and forth? It was the only logical conclusion."

"Sure." Max thought maybe she should just go along with whatever the crazy homicidal maniac had to say.

"Nobody's going to miss her anyway. She was a horrible human being."

"How'd you get back in the shop that night?" Max asked.

"Andy's parents own the building. He has keys to the place."

"Oh, that's right."

"I thought she'd take longer to die. I figured I'd have plenty of time to get the box back before she dropped dead. She must have liked the amaretto cake a lot. I would have brought the water bottle back at the same time, but I had used all the cyanide in the cake. I snuck back in the next day and put it under the desk. It took you forever to find it!"

"Well, now they've found it, and Chad will go to jail for the murder. That's who she got the water from," Max explained.

"Not after they find your suicide note."

"Excuse me?" Max didn't like where this was heading.

"Well, I can't let you live. I figured that you're tortured by guilt over the murder and decide to take your own life."

"Oh, I would never do that."

"The note will be very convincing. I'll tell you what to write."

"Why would I write what you tell me to when I know you're just going to kill me anyway?"

"Oh. I hadn't thought of that." Stacy thought for a moment. "To buy time? You know, a few more minutes of your miserable, boring life. You're such an optimist, I'm sure you expect someone to come crashing through that door and save the day."

That would be great. But, since that wasn't necessarily going to happen, she needed to figure out a way to keep from getting killed. Buying time was a good start.

"So why did you ask me to get involved in the investigation?" Max asked.

"What better way to throw you off the trail, right? And it worked. For a while, anyway." Stacy saw Max's sketch pad and handed it to her. "Sit down."

Max obeyed.

"Now write. Dear friends and family."

"That sounds pretty formal. And I don't really have any family besides my dad. I mean, there's my aunt Vera who lives in Saugus, but we're not especially close."

"Well, what would you write?"

"I think I'd just write 'Dear Dad.' He's the most important person in my life."

"Okay, write Dear Dad."

"But maybe I should include Andy and Eric. Oh, and Keiko."

"I don't care what you write, just write it!" Stacy snapped at her.

Max took her artist pencil and wrote neatly at the top, "Dear Dad, Andy, Eric, and Keiko."

"Now write 'I'm sorry for killing Jennifer.'"

"I don't like the sound of that. How about 'I'm sorry that I killed Jennifer'?"

"Fine! Just write it."

She neatly wrote the sentence.

"Now what?" Max asked.

"Here's what. I'm tired of your stalling." Stacy waved the gun around while she talked. "I'm tired of you. I'm tired of hearing about your stupid lace and your stupid sea glass collection. Everyone just loves you, Max, don't they? Well, I've seen the way you look at my husband. He's clueless, but I'm not. Getting rid of you means I never have to worry about you stealing him away from me. Now, sign it."

"It's not much of a suicide note." Max stared at what she had written, unable to think about what she could do to keep Stacy from killing her.

"I don't care. Just sign it."

Max looked up to see the gun pointed straight at her. She knew as soon as she signed the note, she was dead.

CHAPTER 18

*M*ax remembered the stone in her pocket. Was it possible that there was one wish left? She reached into her pocket to rub it and felt her seam ripper. Her heart started beating even faster. She slipped the cap off of it and wrapped her hand around it.

"Okay, just let me write 'I love you,'" she said, pointing to the pad. As she'd hoped, Stacy's eyes followed where she pointed, and in that moment, she jabbed the seam ripper into Stacy's thigh. She yelped and dropped the gun, pulling the seam ripper out of her leg. Max kicked the gun out of the way and tripped Stacy as she turned to go after it.

Max was never so happy to hear her door jingle. Stacy crawled toward the gun but froze when she looked up and saw Detective Cruz pointing a gun at her.

"She killed Jennifer!" Max shouted.

Stacy stood up quickly. "She's lying! She did it! She was going to kill me too."

"Right," the detective said. "You shouldn't have used chocolate cake when you switched the boxes. If you hadn't, you might have gotten away with murder." He handcuffed Stacy and led her outside. Max heard sirens and then screeching tires as two patrol cars pulled up in front of her shop.

Detective Cruz walked back into her shop. Max stood in the middle of the room, not moving.

"Sit down," he told her and eased her into an armchair. "Are you all right?"

"I'm not sure," she said. "She's a murderer!"

He took his jacket off and wrapped it around her shoulders.

"I thought she was too dumb to be a murderer." The jacket smelled nice. "I guess she got me there."

"She wasn't that bright. She didn't even lock the door."

"How did you know to come here?" she asked. She wanted to hug him. He saved her life! She was alive!

"When I called back and you didn't answer the phone, I got worried. Thanks for not staying out of it," he said.

"What? Oh, you mean the chocolate cake."

"Yeah, that." He sat down across from her. "And the rest of it. This is a small town, Max. Everyone knows what everyone is doing. Three different people told me you were investigating the murder."

"And you didn't want me to interfere."

He took her hands in his. "I didn't want you to get

hurt. After all, I just found you. I'm not ready to lose you."

Max stared into his green eyes and melted. She was probably in shock. He probably said, "I'm not ready to use you." No, that didn't make any sense.

"I'll need a statement," he told her, letting go of her hands. "But we can put it off until tomorrow. Do you want me to call your dad?"

A sixty-something woman in cat-eye glasses and a tracksuit bolted through the door. She seemed familiar.

"You're the one who took the pictures the night of the murder," Max said.

"Gabrielle Darling." She reached out her hand to shake Max's. "I'm with the *Daily Breeze*. Did you like the description of the dress? It was exquisite."

"Yes, thank you," Max replied. "Why do you keep showing up when bad things happen?"

"I have a police scanner. Your dad's on his way. I called him before I came."

"You called my dad?"

"Sure. I still had his number from when I did a story on him last year. He's a local celebrity."

"Thanks for calling him." All of a sudden, she felt exhausted. It was tough work solving a murder. And almost getting shot was very draining. Before she knew it her dad was there, then Eric and Olivia arrived. She soon found herself surrounded by all her friends and neighbors fussing over her.

CHAPTER 19

Saturday was a blur. Three brides came in with their entourages to try on dresses. All three found the perfect dress and put in their orders. There wasn't a chance for a break until three o'clock. Max and Keiko sat down in the showroom.

"Is it always like this on Saturdays?" Keiko asked.

"Sometimes worse," Max answered. "Please tell me that was our last appointment for the day?"

"Yes, that was our last appointment. Your dad called and said he was stopping by."

"Hopefully he's bringing food. Did you even get a chance to eat?"

Before Keiko answered, the door jingled, and Richard walked in with two bags.

"I hope there's food in there," Max said.

"Yes, there's food," he told her. He pulled out several submarine sandwiches and put them on the table.

"Darlene doesn't like us to eat in here," Max warned him.

"To heck with Darlene." He laid out plates and napkins. "How often do you solve a murder?"

"I'm too tired to argue." She leaned back in her chair and looked at all the food. "How many people are you feeding, Dad?"

The door jingled and Fiona and Teresa came in. Teresa held Josie. Before the door closed, Eric arrived with his arms full of more bags.

"What is this, a party?" Max asked as Olivia came in the door.

"That's exactly what it is," Eric said, pulling out two bottles of champagne. The other bag had plastic champagne glasses. He popped the first cork and started pouring glasses for everyone except Keiko. When he finished, he pulled out a bottle of sparkling cider for Keiko.

"Where's Andy?" Keiko asked.

"He didn't feel like celebrating," Richard said. "He said he'd talk to you later."

"Poor Andy! He must be heartbroken." Max knew how much he'd loved Stacy. "I can't imagine what he's feeling after finding out his wife is a murderer."

"He's going to take time to heal," Richard said. "All we can do is be there for him."

Max nodded, thinking of her friend. She wasn't sure their friendship would ever be the same, but she would always think of him as her first love.

Richard raised his glass. "Here's to Max. You found the murderer!"

"To Max," everyone said and touched glasses.

"Well, it's more like she found me."

"Don't be modest, Max," Fiona said. "You did excellent detective work."

"That's not all we're celebrating," Richard announced. "Have you told everyone about New York?"

Max looked at her dad and then Keiko, who avoided her eyes.

"Did I jump the gun?" he asked.

"No." Max stood up. "I've told everyone except Fiona and Teresa." She turned to the two women. "I was offered a job as an assistant designer in New York."

Everyone started talking at once.

"Congratulations, Max." Teresa came over and gave her a hug.

"We're going to miss you," Fiona added.

The door jingled and River came in with her mail. "Cool, a party!" he said and handed her the mail.

Her dad poured River a glass of sparkling cider.

"Everyone, please. Can I have your attention?" Max spoke over the noise.

They all stopped talking and waited for her to speak.

"I realized something this week." She looked at everyone smiling at her. Everyone except Keiko, who hadn't looked happy all day. "You are all so important to me. I don't know what I would do without you."

"We'll always be there for you, Max," Fiona said.

"Always," Teresa agreed.

"And Keiko made me realize something else. I am a designer. So, to go to work for someone as an assistant designer, well, wouldn't that be sort of a demotion?"

"What are you saying, Max?" Richard looked at her expectantly.

"I belong right here," she said. She heard a squeal. Keiko ran up to her and threw her arms around her in a big hug.

"Now, I can celebrate." Keiko held up her glass to toast Max.

The End

Or is it a new beginning?

Thank you so much for reading *Murder in White Lace*!

Go to karensuewalker.com to sign up for Karen's Cozy Club.

The next book in the five-book Bridal Shop Cozy Mystery series, ***Murder in Crimson Velvet***, is available now—get your copy now!

Next: MURDER IN CRIMSON VELVET

Max and Keiko agree to help out at their local theater when the costume designer goes into labor days before a big opening.

An actress confides in Max that a psychic predicted her murder. Max brushes it off as superstitious nonsense until the actress falls to her death.

While she investigates, there's a new romance for Max, though she has trouble ignoring how her pulse races every time she's near Detective Cruz.

To see a list of all of my books, or to sign up for Karen's Cozy Club visit karensuewalker.com.

Made in United States
North Haven, CT
07 December 2025

83974294R00135